The Trouble with Sisters

Beezus felt that the biggest trouble with four-year-old Ramona was that she was just plain exasperating. If Ramona drank lemonade through a straw, she blew into the straw as hard as she could to see what would happen. If she played with her finger paints in the front yard, she wiped her hands on the neighbors' cat. That was the exasperating sort of thing Ramona did. And then there was the way she behaved about her favorite book. . . .

Enjoy all of Beverly Cleary's books

FEATURING RAMONA QUIMBY:

Beezus and Ramona

Ramona the Pest

Ramona the Brave

Ramona and Her Father

Ramona and Her Mother

Ramona Quimby, Age 8

Ramona Forever

Ramona's World

FEATURING HENRY HUGGINS:

Henry Huggins

Henry and Beezus

Henry and Ribsy

Henry and the Paper Route

Henry and the Clubhouse

Ribsy

FEATURING RALPH MOUSE:

The Mouse and the Motorcycle

Runaway Ralph

Ralph S. Mouse

MORE GREAT FICTION BY BEVERLY CLEARY:

Ellen Tebbits

Otis Spofford

Fifteen

The Luckiest Girl

Jean and Johnny

Emily's Runaway Imagination

Sister of the Bride

Mitch and Amy

Socks

Dear Mr. Henshaw

Muggie Maggie

Strider

Two Times the Fun

AND DON'T MISS BEVERLY CLEARY'S AUTOBIOGRAPHIES:

A Girl from Yamhill

My Own Two Feet

BeVerLy cLeary

Beezus
and
Ramona

ILLUSTRATED BY
Tracy Dockray

HARPER FESTIVAL
An Imprint of HarperCollinsPublishers

HarperFestival is an imprint of
HarperCollins Publishers.

Library of Congress catalog card number: 2005938676
ISBN 978-0-06-191461-4
Typography by Amy Ryan
10 11 12 13 14   LP/CW   10 9 8 7 6
❖
Revised paperback edition, 2010

Contents

1

Beezus and Her Little Sister

Beatrice Quimby's biggest problem was her little sister Ramona. Beatrice, or Beezus (as everyone called her, because that was what Ramona had called her when she first learned to talk), knew other nine-year-old girls who had little sisters who went to nursery school, but she did not know anyone with a little sister like Ramona.

Beezus felt that the biggest trouble with

four-year-old Ramona was that she was just plain exasperating. If Ramona drank lemonade through a straw, she blew into the straw as hard as she could to see what would happen. If she played with her finger paints in the front yard, she wiped her hands on the neighbors' cat. That was the exasperating sort of thing Ramona did. And then there was the way she behaved about her favorite book.

It all began one afternoon after school when Beezus was sitting in her father's big chair embroidering a laughing teakettle on a pot holder for one of her aunts for Christmas. She was trying to embroider this one neatly, because she planned to give it to Aunt Beatrice, who was Mother's younger sister and Beezus's most special aunt.

With gray thread Beezus carefully outlined the steam coming from the teakettle's spout and thought about her pretty young aunt, who was always so gay and so understanding. No wonder she was Mother's favorite sister. Beezus hoped to be exactly like Aunt Beatrice when she grew up. She wanted to be a fourth-grade teacher and drive a yellow convertible and live in an apartment house with an elevator and a buzzer that opened the front door. Because she was named after Aunt Beatrice, Beezus felt she might be like her in other ways, too.

While Beezus was sewing, Ramona, holding a mouth organ in her teeth, was riding around the living room on her tricycle. Since she needed both hands to steer the tricycle, she could blow in and out on only one note. This made the harmonica sound as if it were groaning *oh dear, oh dear* over and over again.

Beezus tried to pay no attention. She tied a small knot in the end of a piece of red thread to embroider the teakettle's laughing mouth. "Conceal a knot as you would a secret," Grandmother always said.

Inhaling and exhaling into her mouth organ, Ramona closed her eyes and tried to pedal around the coffee table without looking.

"Ramona!" cried Beezus. "Watch where you're going!"

When Ramona crashed into the coffee table, she opened her eyes again. *Oh dear, oh*

dear, moaned the harmonica. Around and around pedaled Ramona, inhaling and exhaling.

Beezus looked up from her pot holder. "Ramona, why don't you play with Bendix for a while?" Bendix was Ramona's favorite doll. Ramona thought Bendix was the most beautiful name in the world.

Ramona took the harmonica out of her mouth. "No," she said. "Read my Scoopy book to me."

"Oh, Ramona, not Scoopy," protested Beezus. "We've read Scoopy so many times."

Instead of answering, Ramona put her harmonica between her teeth again and pedaled around the room, inhaling and exhaling. Beezus had to lift her feet every time Ramona rode by.

The knot in Beezus's thread pulled through the material of her pot holder, and she gave up trying to conceal it as she would a secret and tied a bigger knot. Finally, tired of trying to keep her feet out of Ramona's way, she put down her embroidery. "All right, Ramona," she said. "If I read about Scoopy, will you stop riding your tricycle around the living room and making so much noise?"

"Yes," said Ramona, and climbed off her tricycle. She ran into the bedroom she shared with Beezus and returned with a battered, dog-eared, sticky book, which she handed to Beezus. Then she climbed into the big chair beside Beezus and waited expectantly.

Reflecting that Ramona always managed to get her own way, Beezus gingerly took the book and looked at it with a feeling of great dislike. It was called *The Littlest Steam Shovel*. On the cover was a picture of a steam shovel with big tears coming out of its eyes. How could a steam shovel have eyes, Beezus thought and, scarcely looking at the words, began for what seemed like the hundredth or maybe the thousandth time, "Once there was a little steam shovel named Scoopy. One day Scoopy said, 'I do not want to be a steam shovel. I want to be a bulldozer.'"

"You skipped," interrupted Ramona.

"No, I didn't," said Beezus.

"Yes, you did," insisted Ramona. "You're supposed to say, 'I want to be a *big* bulldozer.'"

"Oh, all right," said Beezus crossly. "'I want to be a big bulldozer.'"

Ramona smiled contentedly and Beezus continued reading. "'G-r-r-r,' said Scoopy, doing his best to sound like a bulldozer."

Beezus read on through Scoopy's failure to be a bulldozer. She read about Scoopy's wanting to be a trolley bus ("Beep-beep," honked Ramona), a locomotive ("A-hooey, a-hooey," wailed Ramona), and a pile driver

("Clunk! Clunk!" shouted Ramona). Beezus was glad when she finally reached the end of the story and Scoopy learned it was best for little steam shovels to be steam shovels. "There!" she said with relief, and closed the book. She always felt foolish trying to make noises like machinery.

"Clunk! Clunk!" yelled Ramona, jumping down from the chair. She pulled her harmonica out of the pocket of her overalls and climbed on her tricycle. *Oh dear, oh dear,* she inhaled and exhaled.

"Ramona!" cried Beezus. "You promised you'd stop if I read Scoopy to you."

"I did stop," said Ramona, when she had taken the harmonica out of her mouth. "Now read it again."

"Ramona Geraldine Quimby!" Beezus began, and stopped. It was useless to argue with Ramona. She wouldn't pay any attention. "Why do you like that story anyway?"

Beezus asked. "Steam shovels can't talk, and I feel silly trying to make all those noises."

"*I* don't," said Ramona, and wailed, "A-hooey, a-hooey," with great feeling before she put her harmonica back in her mouth.

Beezus watched her little sister pedal furiously around the living room, inhaling and exhaling. Why did she have to like a book about a steam shovel anyway? Girls weren't supposed to like machinery. Why couldn't she like something quiet, like *Peter Rabbit*?

Mother, who had bought *The Littlest Steam Shovel* at the Supermarket to keep Ramona quiet while she shopped one afternoon, was so tired of Scoopy that she always managed to be too busy to read to Ramona. Father came right out and said he was fed up with frustrated steam shovels and he would not read that book to Ramona and, furthermore, no one else was to read it to her while he was in the house. And that was that.

So only Beezus was left to read Scoopy to Ramona. Plainly something had to be done and it was up to Beezus to do it. But what? Arguing with Ramona was a waste of time. So was appealing to her better nature. The best thing to do with Ramona, Beezus had learned, was to think up something to take the place of whatever her mind was fixed upon. And what could take the place of *The Littlest Steam Shovel*? Another book, of course, a better book, and the place to find it was certainly the library.

"Ramona, how would you like me to take you to the library to find a different book?" Beezus asked. She really enjoyed taking Ramona places, which, of course, was quite different from wanting to go someplace herself and having Ramona insist on tagging along.

For a moment Ramona was undecided. Plainly she was torn between wanting *The*

Littlest Steam Shovel read aloud again and the pleasure of going out with Beezus. "O.K.," she agreed at last.

"Get your sweater while I tell Mother," said Beezus.

"Clunk! Clunk!" shouted Ramona happily.

When Ramona appeared with her sweater, Beezus stared at her in dismay. Oh, no, she thought. She can't wear those to the library.

On her head Ramona wore a circle of cardboard with two long paper ears attached. The insides of the ears were colored with pink crayon, Ramona's work at nursery school. "I'm the Easter bunny," announced Ramona.

"Mother," wailed Beezus. "You aren't going to let her wear those awful ears to the library!"

"Why, I don't see why not." Mother

sounded surprised that Beezus should object to Ramona's ears.

"They look so silly. Whoever heard of an Easter bunny in September?" Beezus complained, as Ramona hopped up and down to make her ears flop. I just hope we don't meet anyone we know, Beezus thought, as they started out the front door.

But the girls had no sooner left the house when they saw Mrs. Wisser, a lady who lived in the next block, coming toward them with a friend. It was too late to turn back. Mrs. Wisser had seen them and was waving.

"Why, hello there, Beatrice," Mrs. Wisser said, when they met. "I see you have a dear little bunny with you today."

"Uh . . . yes." Beezus didn't know what else to say.

Ramona obligingly hopped up and down to make her ears flop.

Mrs. Wisser said to her friend, as if Beezus

and Ramona couldn't hear, "Isn't she adorable?"

Both children knew whom Mrs. Wisser was talking about. If she had been talking about Beezus, she would have said something quite different. Such a nice girl, probably. A sweet child. Adorable, never.

"Just look at those eyes," said Mrs. Wisser.

Ramona beamed. She knew whose eyes they were talking about. Beezus knew, too, but she didn't care. Mother said blue eyes were just as pretty as brown.

Mrs. Wisser leaned over to Ramona. "What color are your eyes, sweetheart?" she asked.

"Brown and white," said Ramona promptly.

"Brown and white eyes!" exclaimed the friend. "Isn't that cunning?"

Beezus had thought it was cunning the first time she heard Ramona say it, about a year ago. Since then she had given up trying to explain to Ramona that she wasn't supposed to say she had brown and white eyes, because Ramona always answered, "My eyes *are* brown and white," and Beezus had to admit that, in a way, they were.

"And what is the little bunny's name?" asked Mrs. Wisser's friend.

"My name is Ramona Geraldine Quimby," answered Ramona, and then added generously, "My sister's name is Beezus."

"Beezus!" exclaimed the lady. "What an odd name. Is it French?"

"Oh, no," said Beezus. Wishing, as she so often did, that she had a more common nickname, like Betty or Patsy, she explained as quickly as she could how she happened to be called Beezus.

Ramona did not like to lose the attention of her audience. She hitched up the leg of her overalls and raised her knee. "See my scab?" she said proudly. "I fell down and hurt my knee and it bled and bled."

"Ramona!" Beezus was horrified. "You aren't supposed to show people your scabs."

"Why?" asked Ramona. That was one of the most exasperating things about

Ramona. She never seemed to understand what she was not supposed to do.

"It's a very nice scab," said Mrs. Wisser's friend, but she did not look as if she really thought it was nice.

"Well, we must be going," said Mrs. Wisser.

"Good-by, Mrs. Wisser," said Beezus politely, and hoped that if they met anyone else they knew she could somehow manage to hide Ramona behind a bush.

"By-by, Ramona," said Mrs. Wisser.

"Good-by," said Ramona, and Beezus knew that she felt that a girl who was four years old was too grown up to say by-by.

Except for holding Ramona's hand crossing streets, Beezus lingered behind her the rest of the way to the library. She hoped that all the people who stopped and smiled at Ramona would not think they were together. When they reached the Glenwood Branch Library, she said, "Ramona, wouldn't you like me to carry your ears for you now?"

"No," said Ramona flatly.

Inside the library, Beezus hurried

Ramona into the boys and girls' section and seated her on a little chair in front of the picture books. "See, Ramona," she whispered, "here's a book about a duck. Wouldn't you like that?"

"No," said Ramona in a loud voice.

Beezus's face turned red with embarrassment when everyone in the library looked at Ramona's ears and smiled. "Sh-h," she whispered, as Miss Greever, the grown-ups' librarian, frowned in their direction. "You're supposed to speak quietly in the library."

Beezus selected another book. "Look, Ramona. Here's a funny story about a kitten that falls into the goldfish bowl. Wouldn't you like that?"

"No," said Ramona in a loud whisper. "I want to find my own book."

If only Miss Evans, the children's librarian, were there! She would know how to select a book for Ramona. Beezus noticed Miss

Greever glance disapprovingly in their direction while the other grown-ups watched Ramona and smiled. "All right, you can look," Beezus agreed, to keep Ramona quiet. "I'll go find a book for myself."

When Beezus had selected her book, she returned to the picture-book section, where she found Ramona sitting on the bench with both arms clasped around a big flat book. "I found my book," she said, and held it up for Beezus to see. On the cover was a picture of a steam shovel with its jaws full of rocks. The title was *Big Steve the Steam Shovel*.

"Oh, Ramona," whispered Beezus in dismay. "You don't want that book."

"I do, too," insisted Ramona, forgetting to whisper. "You told me I could pick out my own book."

Under the disapproving stare of Miss Greever, Beezus gave up. Ramona was right. Beezus looked with distaste at the big orange-colored book in its stout library binding. At least it would be due in two weeks, but Beezus did not feel very happy at the thought of two more weeks of steam shovels. And it just went to show how Ramona always got her own way.

Beezus took her book and Ramona's to Miss Greever's desk.

"Is this where you pay for the books?" asked Ramona.

"We don't have to pay for the books," said Beezus.

"Are you going to charge them?" Ramona asked.

Beezus pulled her library card out of her sweater pocket. "I show this card to the lady and she lets us keep the books for two weeks. A library isn't like a store, where you buy things."

Ramona looked as if she did not understand. "I want a card," she said.

"You have to be able to write your own name before you can have a library card," Beezus explained.

"I can write my name," said Ramona.

"Oh, Ramona," said Beezus, "you can't, either."

"Perhaps she really does know how to write her name," said Miss Greever, as she took a card out of her desk. Beezus watched doubtfully while Miss Greever asked Ramona her name and age. Then the librarian asked Ramona what her father's occupation was. When Ramona didn't understand, she asked, "What kind of work does your father do?"

"He mows the lawn," said Ramona promptly.

The librarian laughed. "I mean, how does he earn his living?"

Somehow Beezus did not like to have Miss Greever laugh at her little sister. After all, how could Ramona be expected to know what Father did? "He works for Pacific Gas and Electric Company," Beezus told the librarian.

Miss Greever wrote this down on the card and shoved it across the desk to Ramona. "Write your name on this line," she directed.

Nothing daunted, Ramona grasped the pencil in her fist and began to write. She bore down so hard that the tip snapped off the lead, but she wrote on. When she laid down the pencil, Beezus picked up the card to see what she had written. The line on the card was filled with

"That's my name," said Ramona proudly.
"That's just scribbling," Beezus told her.
"It is too my name," insisted Ramona,

while Miss Greever quietly dropped the card into the wastebasket. "I've watched you write and I know how."

"Here, Ramona, you can hold my card." Beezus tried to be comforting. "You can pretend it's yours."

Ramona brightened at this, and Miss Greever checked out the books on Beezus's card. As soon as they got home, Ramona demanded, "Read my new book to me."

And so Beezus began. "Big Steve was a steam shovel. He was the biggest steam shovel in the whole city. . . ." When she finished the book she had to admit she liked Big Steve better than Scoopy. His only sound effects were tooting and growling. He tooted and growled in big letters on every page. Big Steve did not shed tears or want to be a pile driver. He worked hard at being a steam shovel, and by the end of the book Beezus had learned a lot about steam shovels. Unfortunately, she did not want to learn about steam shovels. Oh, well, she guessed she could stand two weeks of Big Steve.

"Read it again," said Ramona enthusiastically. "I like Big Steve. He's better than Scoopy."

"How would you like me to show you how to really write your name?" Beezus asked, hoping to divert Ramona from steam shovels.

"O.K.," agreed Ramona.

Beezus found pencil and paper and wrote *Ramona* in large, careful letters across the top of the paper.

Ramona studied it critically. "I don't like it," she said at last.

"But that's the way your name is spelled," Beezus explained.

"You didn't make dots and lines," said Ramona. Seizing the pencil, she wrote,

"But, Ramona, you don't understand." Beezus took the pencil and wrote her own name on the paper. "You've seen me write *Beatrice*, which has an *i* and a *t* in it. See, like

25

that. You don't have an *i* or a *t* in your name, because it isn't spelled that way."

Ramona looked skeptical. She grabbed the pencil again and wrote with a flourish,

(handwritten scribble of dots and lines)

"That's my name, because I like it," she announced. "I like to make dots and lines." Lying flat on her stomach on the floor she proceeded to fill the paper with *i*'s and *t*'s.

"But, Ramona, nobody's name is spelled with just . . ." Beezus stopped. What was the use? Trying to explain spelling and writing to Ramona was too complicated. Everything became difficult when Ramona was around, even an easy thing like taking a book out of the library. Well, if Ramona was happy thinking her name was spelled with *i*'s and *t*'s, she could go ahead and think it.

The next two weeks were fairly peaceful.

Mother and Father soon tired of tooting and growling and, like Beezus, they looked forward to the day *Big Steve* was due at the library. Father even tried to hide the book behind the radio, but Ramona soon found it. Beezus was happy that one part of her plan had worked—Ramona had forgotten *The Littlest Steam Shovel* now that she had a better book. On Ramona's second trip to the library, perhaps Miss Evans could find a book that would make her forget steam shovels entirely.

As for Ramona, she was perfectly happy. She had three people to read aloud a book she liked, and she spent much of her time covering sheets of paper with *i*'s and *t*'s. Sometimes she wrote in pencil, sometimes she wrote in crayon, and once she wrote in ink until her mother caught her at it.

Finally, to the relief of the rest of the family, the day came when *Big Steve* had to be returned. "Come on, Ramona," said Beezus. "It's time to go to the library for another book."

"I have a book," said Ramona, who was lying on her stomach writing her version of her name on a piece of paper with purple crayon.

"No, it belongs to the library," Beezus explained, glad that for once Ramona couldn't possibly get her own way.

"It's my book," said Ramona, crossing several *t*'s with a flourish.

"Beezus is right, dear," observed Mother. "Run along and get *Big Steve*."

Ramona looked sulky, but she went into the bedroom. In a few minutes she appeared with *Big Steve* in her hand and a satisfied expression on her face. "It's my book," she announced. "I wrote my name in it."

Mother looked alarmed. "What do you mean, Ramona? Let me see." She took the book and opened it. Every page in the book was covered with enormous purple *i*'s and *t*'s in Ramona's very best handwriting.

"Mother!" cried Beezus. "Look what she's done! And in crayon so it won't erase."

"Ramona Quimby," said Mother. "You're a very naughty girl! Why did you do a thing like that?"

"It's my book," said Ramona stubbornly. "I like it."

"Mother, what am I going to do?" Beezus demanded. "It's checked out on my card and I'm responsible. They won't let me take any more books out of the library, and I won't have anything to read, and it will all be Ramona's fault. She's always spoiling my fun and it isn't fair!" Beezus didn't know what she would do without her library card. She couldn't get along without library books. She just couldn't, that was all.

"I do *not* spoil your fun," stormed

Ramona. "You have all the fun. I can't read and it isn't fair." Ramona's words ended in a howl as she buried her face in her mother's skirt.

"I couldn't read when I was your age and I didn't have someone to read to me all the

time, so it is too fair," argued Beezus. "You always get your own way, because you're the youngest."

"I do not!" shouted Ramona. "And you don't read all the time. You're mean!"

"I am *not* mean," Beezus shouted back.

"Children!" cried Mother. "Stop it, both of you! Ramona, you were a very naughty girl!" A loud sniff came from Ramona. "And, Beezus," her mother continued, "the library won't take your card away from you. If you'll get my purse I'll give you some money to pay for the damage to the book. Take Ramona along with you, explain what happened, and the librarian will tell you how much to pay."

This made Beezus feel better. Ramona sulked all the way to the library, but when they got there Beezus was pleased to see that Miss Evans, the children's librarian, was sitting behind the desk. Miss Evans was the kind of librarian who would understand about little sisters.

"Hello, Beatrice," said Miss Evans. "Is this your little sister I've heard so much about?"

Beezus wondered what Miss Evans had heard about Ramona. "Yes, this is Ramona," she said and went on hesitantly, "and, Miss Evans, she—"

"I'm a bad girl," interrupted Ramona, smiling winningly at the librarian.

"Oh, you are?" said Miss Evans. "What did you do?"

"I wrote in a book," said Ramona, not the least ashamed. "I wrote in purple crayon and it will never, ever erase. Never, never, never."

Embarrassed, Beezus handed Miss Evans *Big Steve the Steam Shovel.* "Mother gave me the money to pay for the damage," she explained.

The librarian turned the pages of the

book. "Well, you didn't miss a page, did you?" she finally said to Ramona.

"No," said Ramona, pleased with herself. "And it will never, never—"

"I'm awfully sorry," interrupted Beezus. "After this I'll try to keep our library books where she can't reach them."

Miss Evans consulted a file of little cards in a drawer. "Since every page in the book was damaged and the library can no longer use it, I'll have to ask you to pay for the whole book. I'm sorry, but this is the rule. It will cost two dollars and fifty cents."

Two dollars and fifty cents! What a lot of things that would have bought, Beezus reflected, as she pulled three folded dollar bills out of her pocket and handed them to the librarian. Miss Evans put the money in a drawer and gave Beezus fifty cents in change.

Then Miss Evans took a rubber stamp

and stamped something inside the book. By twisting her head around, Beezus could see that the word was *Discarded*. "There!" Miss Evans said, pushing the book across the desk. "You have paid for it, so now it's yours."

Beezus stared at the librarian. "You mean . . . to keep?"

"That's right," answered Miss Evans.

Ramona grabbed the book. "It's mine. I told you it was mine!" Then she turned to Beezus and said triumphantly, "You said people didn't buy books at the library and now you just bought one!"

"Buying a book and paying for damage are not the same thing," Miss Evans pointed out to Ramona.

Beezus could see that Ramona didn't care. The book was hers, wasn't it? It was paid for and she could keep it. And that's not fair, thought Beezus. Ramona shouldn't get her own way when she had been naughty.

"But, Miss Evans," protested Beezus, "if she spoils a book she shouldn't get to keep it. Now every time she finds a book she likes she will ..." Beezus did not go on. She knew very well what Ramona would do, but she wasn't going to say it out loud in front of her.

"I see what you mean." Miss Evans looked thoughtful. "Give me the book, Ramona," she said.

Doubtfully Ramona handed her the book.

"Ramona, do you have a library card?" Miss Evans asked.

Ramona shook her head.

"Then Beezus must have taken the book out on her card," said Miss Evans. "So the book belongs to Beezus."

Why, of course! Why hadn't she thought of that before? It was her book, not Ramona's.

"Oh, thank you," said Beezus gratefully, as Miss Evans handed the book to her. She could do anything she wanted with it.

For once Ramona didn't know what to say. She scowled and looked as if she were building up to a tantrum. "You've got to read it to me," she said at last.

"Not unless I feel like it," said Beezus. "After all, it's my book," she couldn't resist adding.

"That's no fair!" Ramona looked as if she were about to howl.

"It is too fair," said Beezus calmly. "And if you have a tantrum I won't read to you at all."

Suddenly, as if she had decided Beezus meant what she said, Ramona stopped scowling. "O.K.," she said cheerfully.

Beezus watched her carefully for a minute. Yes, she really was being agreeable, thought Beezus with a great feeling of relief.

And now that she did not have to read *Big Steve* unless she wanted to, Beezus felt she would not mind reading it once in a while. "Come on, Ramona," she said. "Maybe I'll have time to read to you before Father comes home."

"O.K.," said Ramona happily, as she took Beezus's hand.

Miss Evans smiled at the girls as they started to leave. "Good luck, Beatrice," she said.

2

Beezus and
Her Imagination

Beezus and Ramona both looked forward to Friday afternoons after school—Beezus because she attended the art class in the recreation center in Glenwood Park, Ramona because she was allowed to go to the park with Beezus and play in the sand pile until the class was over. This Friday while Beezus held Ramona by the hand and waited for the traffic light to change from red to green, she thought how wonderful it would be to have an imagination like Ramona's.

"Oh, you know Ramona. Her imagination runs away with her," Mother said, when Ramona made up a story about seeing a fire engine crash into a garbage truck.

"That child has an imagination a mile long," the Quimbys' grown-up friends remarked when Ramona sat in the middle of the living-room floor in a plastic wading pool she had dragged up from the basement and pretended she was in a boat in the middle of the lake.

"Did you ever see so much imagination in such a little girl?" the neighbors asked one another when Ramona hopped around the yard pretending she was the Easter bunny.

One spring day Ramona had got lost, because she started out to find the pot of gold at the end of the rainbow. The rainbow had appeared to end in the park until she reached the park, but then it looked as if it ended behind the Supermarket. When the police brought Ramona home, Father said, "Sometimes I think Ramona has too much imagination."

Nobody, reflected Beezus, ever says anything about my imagination. Nobody at all. And she wished, more than anything, that she had imagination. How pleased Miss Robbins, the art teacher, would be with her if she had an imagination like Ramona's!

Unfortunately, Beezus was not very good at painting—as least not the way Miss Robbins wanted boys and girls to paint. She wanted them to use their imagination and to feel free. Beezus still squirmed with embarrassment when she thought of her first painting, a picture of a dog with *bowwow* coming out of his mouth in a balloon.

Miss Robbins pointed out that only in the funny papers did dogs have *bowwow* coming out of their mouths in balloons. *Bowwow* in a balloon was not art. When Miss Robbins did think one of Beezus's paintings was good enough to put up on the wall, she always tacked it way down at the end, never in the center. Beezus wished she could have a painting in the center of the wall.

"Hurry up, Ramona," Beezus coaxed. Then she noticed that her sister was dragging a string along behind her. "Oh, Ramona," she protested, "why did you have to bring Ralph with you?" Ralph was an imaginary green lizard Ramona liked to pretend she was leading by a string.

"I love Ralph," said Ramona firmly, "and Ralph likes to go to the park."

Beezus knew it was easier to pretend along with Ramona than to make her stop. Anyway, it was better to have her pretend to

lead a lizard than to pretend to be a lizard herself. "Can't you carry him?" she suggested.

"No," said Ramona. "He's slimy."

When the girls came to the shopping district, Ramona had to stop at the drugstore scales and pretend to weigh herself while Beezus held Ralph's string. "I weigh fifty-eleven pounds," she announced, while Beezus smiled at Ramona's idea of her weight. It just goes to show how much imagination Ramona has, she thought.

At the radio-and-phonograph store Ramona insisted on petting His Master's Voice, the black-and-white plaster dog, bigger than Ramona, that always sat with one ear cocked in front of the door. Beezus thought admiringly about the amount of imagination it took to pretend that a scarred and chipped plaster dog was real. If only she had an imagination like Ramona's, maybe Miss Robbins would say her paintings were free and imaginative and would tack them on the middle of the wall.

When they reached the park, Beezus left Ramona and Ralph at the sand pile and, feeling more and more discouraged at her own lack of imagination, hurried to the recreation center. The class had already poured paints into their muffin tins and were painting on paper thumbtacked to drawing boards. The room hummed with activity. Miss Robbins, wearing a gay paint-smeared smock, flew from one artist to another, praising, correcting, suggesting.

Beezus waited until Miss Robbins finished explaining to a boy that he should not outline a mouth with black paint. Her mouth wasn't outlined in black, was it? Then Beezus said, "I'm sorry I'm late, Miss Robbins." She stared in fascination at Miss Robbins's earrings. They came almost to her shoulders and were made of silver wire twisted and bent into interesting shapes— not the shape of anything in particular, just interesting shapes.

"That's all right." Miss Robbins, her earrings swinging, smiled at Beezus. "Get your paints and paper. Today everyone is painting an imaginary animal."

"An imaginary animal?" Beezus repeated blankly. How could she possibly think of an imaginary animal? As Beezus poured paints into her muffin tin and tacked a sheet of paper to her drawing board, she tried to think of an imaginary animal, but all the animals she could think of—cats and dogs, cows and horses, lions and giraffes—were discouragingly real.

Reluctantly Beezus took the only vacant seat, which was beside a boy named Wayne who came to the class only because his mother made him. Once Beezus had hung her sweater on the back of a chair, and Wayne had printed "Post No Bills" on it in chalk. Beezus had worn it all the way home before she discovered it. Since then she did not care to sit beside Wayne. Today she noticed he had parked a grape-flavored lollipop on a paper towel beside his muffin tin of paints.

"Hi, Beez," he greeted her. "No fair licking my sucker."

"I don't want your old sucker," answered Beezus. "And don't call me Beez."

"O.K., Beez," said Wayne.

At that moment the door opened and Ramona walked into the room. She was still dragging the string behind her and she looked angry.

"Why, hello," said Miss Robbins pleasantly.

"Oh, Ramona, you're supposed to be playing in the sand pile," said Beezus, going over to her.

"No," said Ramona flatly. "Howie threw sand on Ralph." Her dark eyes were busy taking in the paints, the brushes, the drawing boards. "I'm going to paint," she announced.

"Mother said you were supposed to play in the sand pile," protested Beezus. "You're too little for this class."

"You say that about everything," complained Ramona. Then she turned to Miss Robbins. "Don't step on Ralph," she said.

"Ralph is a make-believe green lizard she pretends she leads around on a string." Beezus was embarrassed at having to explain such a silly thing.

Miss Robbins laughed. "Well, here is a little girl with lots of imagination. How would you like to paint a picture of Ralph for us, Ramona?"

Beezus could not help feeling annoyed. Miss Robbins was letting Ramona stay in the class—the one place where she was never allowed to tag along! Miss Robbins would probably like her painting, because it would be so full of imagination. Ramona's pictures, in fact, were so full of imagination that it took even more imagination to tell what they were.

Ramona beamed at Miss Robbins, who found a drawing board for her and a stool, which she placed between Beezus and Wayne. She lifted Ramona onto the stool. "There. Now you can share your sister's paints," she said.

Ramona looked impressed at being allowed to paint with such big boys and girls. She sat quietly on her stool, watching everything around her.

Maybe she'll behave herself after all, thought Beezus as she dipped her brush into blue paint, and now I don't have to sit next to Wayne. Since Beezus still had not thought of an imaginary animal, she decided to start with the sky.

"Do the sky first," Beezus whispered to Ramona, who looked as if she did not know how to begin. Then Beezus faced her own work, determined to be free and imaginative. To be free on a piece of paper was not

as easy as it sounded, she thought. Miss Robbins always said to start with the big areas of a picture and paint them bravely and boldly, so Beezus spread the sky on her paper with brave, bold strokes. Back and forth across the paper she swept her brush. Brave and bold and free—that was the way to do it.

Her sky turned out to be too wet, so while it dried a little, Beezus looked at what the other boys and girls were doing. Celia, who sat on her left, had already filled in a brave, bold background of pink, which she had sprinkled with big purple dots. Now she was painting a long gray line that wound all over her paper, in and out around the dots.

"What's that supposed to be?" whispered Beezus.

"I'm not sure yet," answered Celia.

Beezus felt better, because Celia was the kind of girl who usually knew exactly what she was doing and whose pictures were often tacked in the center of the wall. The boy on the other side of Celia, who always wanted to paint airplanes, was painting what looked like a giraffe made of pieces of machinery, and another boy was painting a thing that had two heads.

Beezus looked across Ramona to Wayne. He had not bothered with a sky at all. He had painted a hen. Beezus knew it was a hen, because he had printed in big letters, "This is a real hen," with an arrow pointing to it. Wayne always tried to do just the opposite of what Miss Robbins wanted.

"Hey, quit peeking," said Wayne in a loud voice.

"I'm not peeking," said Beezus, hastily trying to look as if she had been interested in Ramona's paper all the time.

Ramona had dipped her brush into blue paint and had painted a blue stripe across the top of her paper. "That's the sky," she said happily.

"But that's not the way the sky is." Beezus was trying to be helpful. She felt better, because Ramona had not plunged in and painted a picture full of imagination. "Skies should come farther down on the paper."

"The sky is up," said Ramona firmly.

Beezus decided she couldn't waste time explaining about skies, not when she still hadn't thought of an imaginary animal. Maybe she could take a real animal and sort of change it around. Let's see, she thought, I could take a horse and put feathers on it. No, all those feathers would be too hard to paint. Wings? That was it! A horse with wings was an imaginary animal—a real imaginary animal—because Mother had once read aloud a story about Pegasus, the winged horse, out of a library book. In the story Pegasus had been white, which was a real horse color. Beezus decided to be extra-imaginative. She would make her horse green—a green horse against a blue sky. Miss Robbins ought to like that. Beezus did not think blue and green looked very pretty together, but Miss Robbins often liked colors that Beezus thought did not really go together.

Beezus dipped her brush into green paint and outlined a wing against the sky. Next she outlined the body of the horse and a long tail that hung down. It was a magnificent horse. At least, Beezus hoped it would look magnificent when she finished it. Anyway, it was big, because Miss Robbins liked her artists to cover the whole paper. Quickly and neatly Beezus filled in the outline of the horse, because Miss Robbins, who was looking at Celia's picture, would look at hers next. Somehow the horse was not exactly what Beezus had in her mind's eye, but even so, compared to whatever Celia was painting, a green horse with wings was really a very good imaginary animal. And except for a few soggy places in the sky, her work was much neater than Celia's. Beezus waited for Miss Robbins to point this out.

Instead, Miss Robbins said, "Celia, your

picture is work to be proud of. It is a difficult thing to get to be as free as this."

Then Miss Robbins moved on to Beezus, her long earrings swinging forward as she leaned over the drawing board. Beezus waited anxiously. Maybe her picture wasn't so good, after all. If Miss Robbins liked a gray line winding around a lot of purple dots, maybe she wouldn't like a flying horse. Maybe she liked things with no special shape, like those earrings.

"You have a good sky even if it is a little wet," said Miss Robbins.

Beezus was disappointed. Anybody could have a good sky.

Miss Robbins continued to study the picture. "Try to think how a horse would look if it were really flying."

Beezus tried to think.

"What about the tail?" asked Miss Robbins. "Wouldn't the tail fly out behind instead of hanging down?"

"Especially if the wind blew real hard," said Wayne.

"Can't you make the horse look rounder?" asked Miss Robbins. "Think how a horse looks with the sun shining on him. Part of him would be in shadow."

"Not that horse," said Wayne. "She just copied it off a Mobilgas billboard, only she made it green instead of red."

"I did not!" said Beezus indignantly. Then she stared at her painting again. Now that Wayne pointed it out, she could see her horse did look like the one on the Mobilgas billboard at the service station where her father bought gasoline. He was a flat cardboard horse, not a magnificent horse at all. Her horse wasn't even as good as the horse on the billboard, because instead of a flying tail he had a tail that hung down like . . . well, like a mop.

"All right, Wayne," said Miss Robbins. "I'm sure Beezus did not mean to copy anything from a billboard."

"No, I didn't," said Beezus mournfully. "I was only trying to change a real animal around to make it imaginary, but I just don't have imagination, is all."

"Why, Beezus, of course you have imagination!"

Miss Robbins sounded shocked at the idea of anyone's not having imagination.

"My little sister has lots of imagination," said Beezus. "Everybody says so."

Miss Robbins smiled reassuringly. "That doesn't mean that you don't have any. I think your trouble is that you work too hard. You don't have to be so neat. Why don't you start another painting and just try to have a good time with your paints?"

Beezus looked uncertain. It was a nice change to have a grown-up tell her she didn't have to be neat, but she didn't understand how she could paint a good picture unless she worked at it. If only she had some imagination, like Ramona—but no, Miss Robbins said everybody had imagination. Well, if she had imagination, where was it? Why wasn't it helping her with her imaginary animal? All she could think of was that cardboard horse on the billboard.

Beezus glanced at Ramona, who had been surprisingly quiet for a long time, to see how she was coming along with her picture of Ralph. Except for the stripe of sky at the top, Ramona's paper was blank. Now she dipped her brush in yellow paint, divided the hairs of the brush into three tufts, and pressed them on the paper, leaving a mark like the track of a bird.

"That's not the way to use a paint brush," said Beezus. "Besides, you're getting paint on your fingers."

"Look—Ralph's feet marks," exclaimed Ramona, paying no attention to Beezus.

"You mean footprints," corrected Beezus. "Now go on and paint the rest of Ralph."

"Feet marks," said Ramona stubbornly, making more footprints across the paper. "And I can't paint him, because he's just pretend."

Oh, well, thought Beezus, maybe making footprints isn't good for the brush, but it keeps her quiet. She dabbled her own brush in green paint and tried to stir up her imagination. She felt a little encouraged because Ramona was having trouble too.

"Hey!" interrupted Wayne in a loud voice. "She's licking my sucker!"

"Ramona!" Beezus was horrified to see Ramona, no longer interested in footprints, calmly sucking Wayne's grape-flavored lollipop. "Ramona, put that down this instant! You're not supposed to lick other people's suckers."

"You give me that!" Wayne made a grab for his lollipop.

"No!" screamed Ramona, trying to hold it out of his reach. "I want it!"

"Ramona, give it to him," ordered Beezus. "It's all germy."

"You mean she's getting germs on it," said Wayne. "Give it to me!"

The rest of the class stopped painting to watch. Wayne made another grab for his lollipop. This time he grabbed Ramona by the wrist.

"Let go of her!" said Beezus angrily.

Ramona howled as Wayne tried to pry her fingers loose from the lollipop stick. He knocked against his muffin tin, which flipped into the air spattering paint over the table, the drawing boards, and the floor. Ramona was splashed with red and yellow paint. Blue and green ran down Wayne's jeans onto his sneakers. A pool of brown paint dripped off the table onto the floor.

"Now see what you did," said Wayne, after he had pried his sucker out of Ramona's fist.

"See what *you* did," contradicted Beezus. "Picking on my little sister like that!" She picked up the paper towel the sucker had been resting on and began to wipe the spatters off Ramona, who continued to howl.

"Boys and girls!" Miss Robbins raised her voice. "Let's be quiet. When the room is quiet I know you are thinking. Lots of people don't know you have to think while you paint." Then she turned to Wayne. "All right, Wayne, you may get a damp cloth and wipe up the paint."

"I'm sorry, Miss Robbins," said Beezus.

"I want the sucker!" screamed Ramona.

Suddenly Beezus decided she had had enough. This art class was one place where Ramona was not supposed to be. She was supposed to play in the sand pile. Mother had said so. She was not supposed to upset the class and spoil everything with one of her tantrums. Beezus made up her mind she was going to do something about it and right now, too, though she didn't know what.

"Ramona, stop that this instant," Beezus ordered. "Go out and play in the sand pile, where you belong, or I'll . . . I'll . . ." Frantically Beezus tried to think what she could do. Then she had an inspiration. "Or I'll tickle you!" she finished. I guess I do have some imagination, after all, she thought triumphantly.

Instantly Ramona stopped crying. She hugged herself and stared at Beezus. "Don't tickle, Beezus," she begged. "Please don't tickle."

"Then go out and play in the sand pile, like Mother says you're supposed to," said Beezus.

"Don't tickle," shrieked Ramona, as she scrambled down from her stool and ran out the door.

Well! thought Beezus. It worked! It really worked!

Feeling suddenly lighthearted, she tacked

a fresh sheet of paper to her drawing board and sat staring at it. Maybe Ramona didn't have so much imagination after all, if she couldn't draw a picture of an imaginary green lizard. Well, if Ramona couldn't paint a picture of Ralph, *she* could. Ramona was not the only one in the family with imagination. So there!

Beezus seized her brush and painted in another sky with bold, free strokes. Then she dipped her brush into green paint and started to outline a lizard on her paper. Let's see, what did a lizard look like? She could not remember. It didn't matter much, anyway—not for an imaginary animal. She had started the lizard with such brave, bold strokes that it took up most of the paper and looked more like a dragon.

Beezus promptly decided the animal was a dragon. Dragons breathed fire, but she did not have any orange paint, and she was so late in starting this picture that she didn't want to take time to mix any. She dipped her brush into pink paint instead and made flames come out of the dragon's mouth. Only they didn't look like flames. They looked more like the spun-sugar candy Beezus had once eaten at the circus. And a dragon breathing clouds of pink candy was more fun than an ordinary flame-breathing dragon.

Forgetting everyone around her, Beezus made the pink clouds bigger and fluffier. Dragons had pointed things down their backs, so Beezus made a row of spines down the back. They did not look quite right— more like slanting sticks than spines. Lollipop sticks, of course!

At that Beezus laughed to herself. Naturally a dragon that breathed pink spun sugar would have lollipops down its back. Eagerly she dipped her brush into red paint and put a strawberry lollipop on one of the sticks. She painted a different flavor on each stick, finishing with a grape-flavored lollipop like the one Wayne and Ramona had shared.

Then she held her drawing board at arm's length. She was pleased with her dragon. It was funny and colorful and really imaginary. Beezus wondered what she should do next. Then she remembered that Miss Robbins often said it was important for an artist to know when to stop painting. Maybe she'd spoil her picture if she added anything. No, just one more touch. She dipped her brush in yellow paint and gave the dragon an eye—a lemon-drop eye. There! Her imaginary animal was finished!

By that time it was four-thirty and most of the boys and girls had put away their drawing boards and washed their muffin tins. Several mothers who had come for their children were wandering around the room looking at the paintings.

"Those who have finished, wash your hands clean," said Miss Robbins. "And I mean clean." Then she came across the room to Beezus. "Why, Beezus!" she exclaimed. "This is a picture to be proud of!"

"I didn't know whether a dragon should have lollipops down his back or not, but they were fun to paint," said Beezus.

"Of course he can have lollipops down his back. It's a splendid idea. After all, no one has ever seen a dragon, so no one knows how one should look." Miss Robbins turned to several of the mothers and said, with admiration in her voice, "Here's a girl with real imagination."

Beezus smiled modestly at her toes while the mothers admired her picture.

"We'll tack this in the very center of the wall for next week's classes to see," said Miss Robbins.

"It was fun to paint," confided Beezus, her face flushed with pleasure.

"Of course it was," said Miss Robbins, as she carefully placed the picture in the center of the wall. "Didn't I tell you you worked too hard at painting before?"

Beezus nodded. That was the wonderful thing about it, she thought, as she scrubbed out her muffin tins. Her dragon had been fun, while her flying horse had been work. And she had imagination. Maybe not as much as Ramona, but real imagination just the same. "Here's a girl with real imagination," Miss Robbins had said.

A girl with real imagination, a girl with real imagination, Beezus thought as she left the building and ran across the park to the sand pile. "Come on, Ramona, it's time to go home," she called to her little sister, who was happily sprinkling sand on a sleeping dog. "And let's not forget Ralph!" Good old Ralph!

3

Ramona and Ribsy

One day after school Henry Huggins, who lived in the next block, came over to play checkers with Beezus. His dog Ribsy came with him, because Henry never went anywhere without Ribsy. Beezus liked Henry, because she knew he thought she had more sense than most girls, and the two often played checkers together. So far Beezus had won forty-eight games and

Henry had won forty-nine, not counting
the games Ramona had spoiled by tipping
over the checkerboard.

This afternoon Beezus and Henry knelt
on either side of the coffee table with the
checkerboard between them. Ribsy lay on
the rug near Henry and warily watched

Ramona, who was wearing her rabbit ears and riding her tricycle around the living room.

"Your move," said Henry to Beezus.

"I want to play," said Ramona, riding her tricycle up to the coffee table and shaking her head to make her ears flop. Ribsy got up and moved to a corner, where he lay down with his nose on his paws to watch Ramona.

"You're too little," said Beezus, as she moved a checker. "Besides, only two can play checkers."

"We could play tiddlywinks," said Ramona. "I know how to play tiddlywinks."

Beezus did not answer. Her mind was on the game as she watched Henry's move very carefully.

"I said we could play tiddlywinks," yelled Ramona.

Beezus looked up from the checkerboard.

"Ramona, you stop bothering us," she said in her severest voice.

Ramona scowled and pedaled backwards away from the coffee table while Beezus returned to her game and studied the board. She had to be careful, because Henry had already captured half of her checkers. Let's see, she thought, I could move from here to there—no, that wouldn't work, because then he could—but if I move from there to there—yes, that was it! Beezus lifted her hand to pick up the checker.

At that instant Ramona pedaled as fast as she could toward the coffee table. Crash! The front wheel of Ramona's tricycle rammed into the table. Checkers bounced into the air and showered over the table, falling to the floor and rolling across the rug.

"There!" said Ramona, and calmly pedaled away.

"Hey!" protested Henry.

"Mother!" Beezus called. "Ramona's bothering us!"

Wiping her hands on her apron, Mother came out of the kitchen. "Ramona, you know you're not supposed to bother Henry and Beezus when they're playing checkers. Now go to your room and stay there until you are able to behave yourself."

"No," said Ramona. "I don't have anybody to play with me and I want Beezus and Henry to play with me."

"You heard me." Mother lifted Ramona off the tricycle.

I'll bet she has a tantrum, thought Beezus, as she picked up the checkers.

"No!" screamed Ramona.

"Ramona," said Mother in a warning voice, "I'm going to count to ten."

Ramona threw herself on the floor and kicked and screamed.

"One . . . two . . ." began Mother.

Ramona went on kicking and screaming until Mother counted to seven. Then she lay still on the floor, watching to see if Mother really meant what she said.

"Eight . . . nine," said Mother.

Ramona got to her feet, ran into the bedroom, and slammed the door. Mother returned to the kitchen, and Beezus and Henry started a new game as if nothing had happened. Tantrums were not unusual in the Quimby household. Even Henry knew that.

In a few minutes Beezus heard Ramona open the bedroom door. "Now can I come out?" she called.

"Can you stop bothering Beezus and Henry?" Mother asked from the kitchen.

"No," said Ramona, and shut the door.

Not more than one minute later Ramona opened the door again and came into the living room. "I can stop bothering," she said with a sulky look on her face, and Beezus could see she was still cross because she had been punished.

"That's good," called Mother. "Come here, and I'll give you a cookie."

Seeing Ramona go into the kitchen, Ribsy sat up, scratched, and trotted after her. Although Ribsy did not trust Ramona, he was always interested in what went on in a kitchen.

I hope she stays in the kitchen, thought Beezus, as she picked up a checker and skipped from here to there to there and captured two of Henry's men. The game became so exciting that Beezus almost forgot about Ramona. At the same time she was vaguely aware of scuffling sounds in the hall. Then she heard the jingle of Ribsy's license tags and the click of his claws on the hardwood floor. Ribsy gave a short bark. Then the bathroom door slammed. I wonder what Ramona is doing, thought Beezus, as she captured another checker, but she did not much care so long as Ramona did not interrupt the game.

"Let me in!" screamed Ramona from the hall. "Let me in the bathroom."

"Ramona, who are you talking to?" asked Mother as she went into the hall.

"Ribsy," said Ramona, and beat on the door with her fists.

Ribsy began to bark. From behind the bathroom door his barks made a hollow, echoing sound. Puzzled, Henry looked at Beezus. Ribsy in the bathroom? Henry decided he had better investigate. Reluctantly Beezus left the game and followed him into the hall.

"Open the door and let him out," said Mother.

"I can't," shouted Ramona angrily, above Ribsy's furious barks. "The bad old dog went and locked the door."

"Oh, stop pretending." Beezus was exasperated with Ramona for interrupting the game a second time. It was too bad that a girl couldn't have a friend over for a game of checkers without her little sister spoiling all her fun.

"I'm not pretending," screamed Ramona,

clinging to the doorknob while Ribsy barked and scratched at the other side of the door.

"Ramona!" Mother's voice was stern. "Let that dog out."

"I can't," cried Ramona, rattling the bathroom door. "The bad old dog locked me out."

"Nonsense. Dogs can't lock doors," scolded Mother. "Now open that door and let him out."

Ramona began to sob and Ribsy barked louder. Ramona gave the door a good hard kick.

"Oh, for Pete's sake," muttered Henry.

"Ramona, I am very cross with you," said Mother. She pried Ramona's fingers loose and started to open the door. The knob would not turn. "That's strange," she remarked, and rattled the door herself. Then she hit the door with her fist to see if it might be stuck.

The door did not budge. There was no doubt about it. The bathroom door was locked.

"But how could it be locked?" Henry asked.

"I told you Ribsy locked it," Ramona shouted.

"Don't be silly," said Beezus impatiently.

"Now how on earth—" began Mother in a puzzled voice and then she interrupted herself. "Do you suppose when Ribsy was pawing at the door he bumped against the button in the center of the knob and really did lock the door? Of course! That's exactly what must have happened."

A dog that locked the bathroom door! That Ribsy, thought Beezus. He's always getting into trouble, and now he's locked the Quimbys out of their bathroom.

"I told you he locked the door," Ramona said.

"Yes, but what was my dog doing in the bathroom in the first place?" Henry demanded.

"I put him there," said Ramona.

"Ramona Quimby!" Even Mother sounded exasperated. "Sometimes I don't know what gets into you. You know dogs don't belong in the bathroom. Now go to your room and stay there until I tell you to come out."

"Yes, but—" Ramona began.

"I don't want to have to speak to you again." It was unusual for Mother to be as stern as this.

Still crying, Ramona went to her room, which was next to the bathroom. Since Mother had not told her to close the door, Ramona stood just inside it and waited to see what would happen next.

"Where is the key?" Beezus asked.

"I don't know," answered Mother. "I don't

remember that we ever had a key."

"But there's a keyhole," said Beezus. "There must be a key."

"Ribsy, be quiet," ordered Henry. "We'll get you out." But Ribsy only barked harder, and his barks echoed and re-echoed around the small room.

"No one gave us a key to the bathroom when we rented the house," explained Mother. "And when Ramona first learned to walk we fastened the button down with Scotch tape so she couldn't lock herself in."

"You did?" Ramona, fascinated with this bit of information about herself, stopped crying and leaned out into the hall. "How big was I then?" No one bothered to answer her.

"We've got to get Ribsy out of the bathroom," said Beezus.

"Yes," agreed Mother, "but how?"

"If you have a ladder I'll climb in the

bathroom window and unlock the door," Henry offered.

"The window is locked too," said Mother, bending over to examine the knob on the door.

"Maybe we could call the fire department." Henry tried another suggestion. "They're always rescuing cats and things."

"They couldn't do anything with the bathroom window locked," Beezus pointed out.

"I guess that's right." Henry sounded disappointed. It would have been exciting to have the fire department rescue Ribsy.

"Well, I just can't see any way to take the knob off," said Mother. "There aren't any screws on this side of the door."

"We've got to get him out some way," said Henry. "We can't leave him in there. He'll get hungry."

Beezus did not think this remark of

Henry's was very thoughtful. Of course Ribsy would get hungry if he stayed in the bathroom long enough, but on the other hand they would need their bathroom and it was Henry's dog who had locked them out. Then Beezus made a suggestion. "Maybe if we pushed some glue under the door so Ribsy would get his paws in it, and then called to him so he would scratch at the door, maybe his paws would stick to the button in the knob and he could unlock it himself." Beezus thought her idea was a good one until she saw the disgusted look on Henry's face. "I just thought it might work," she said apologetically.

"Mother—" began Ramona, leaning out into the hall.

Mother paid no attention to her. "I just don't see what we can do—"

"*Mother,*" said Ramona urgently. This time she stepped into the hall.

"Unless we get a ladder (Go back to your room, Ramona) and break the window so we can unlock it," Mother continued, speaking with one sentence inside another, the way grown-ups so often did with Ramona around.

"But *Mother,*" insisted Ramona even more urgently. "I have to——"

"Oh, dear, I might have known," sighed Mother. "Well, come on. I'll take you next door."

Leave it to Ramona, thought Beezus, embarrassed to have her little sister behave this way in front of Henry.

"Don't worry, Ribsy," said Henry. "We'll get you out somehow." He turned to Beezus and said gloomily, "If we don't get him out by dinnertime, maybe we could cut some meat up in real little pieces and shove it under the door to him. I don't see how we could get a drink of water to him, though."

"We have to get him out before then," said Beezus. "Father wouldn't like it if he came home and found Ribsy had locked him out of the bathroom."

"Ribsy couldn't have locked the door if Ramona hadn't put him in the bathroom in the first place," Henry pointed out. "What a dumb thing to do!"

Beezus had nothing to say to this. What could she say when it really had been Ramona's fault?

Mother and Ramona soon returned. "I think we'll get Ribsy out now," said Mother cheerfully. "The lady next door says her little grandson locks himself in the bathroom every time he comes to visit her, and she always unlocks the door with a nail file. She told me how to do it." Mother found a nail file, which she inserted in the keyhole. She wiggled it around, the doorknob clicked, and Mother opened the door. It was as easy as that!

With a joyous bark Ribsy bounded out and jumped up on Henry. "Good old Ribsy," said Henry. "Did you think we were going to leave you in there?" Ribsy wriggled and wagged his tail happily because he was free at last.

"Now maybe he'll be a good dog," said Ramona sulkily.

"He is a good dog, aren't you, Ribsy?" Henry patted him.

"He is *not* a good dog," contradicted Ramona. "He took my cookie away from me and gobbled it right up."

"Oh," said Henry uncomfortably. "I didn't know he ate your cookie."

"Well, he did," said Ramona, "and I made him go in the bathroom until he could be a good dog."

From the way Henry looked at Ramona, Beezus could tell he didn't think much of her reason for shutting Ribsy in the bathroom.

"Oh, Ramona." Mother looked amused and exasperated at the same time. "Just because you were sent to your room is no reason for you to try to punish Henry's dog."

"It is, too," said Ramona defiantly. "He was bad."

"Well, I guess I better be going," said Henry. "Come on, Ribsy."

"Don't go, Henry," begged Beezus. "Maybe we could go out on the porch or someplace and play a game."

"Some other time maybe," answered Henry. "I've got things to do."

"All right," agreed Beezus reluctantly. Henry probably knew they wouldn't be safe from Ramona anywhere, the way she was behaving today.

When Henry had gone, Ramona gave a hop to make her rabbit ears flop. "*Now* we can play tiddlywinks!" she announced, as if she had been waiting for this moment all afternoon.

"No, we can't," snapped Beezus, who could not remember when she had been so annoyed with Ramona.

"Yes, we can," said Ramona. "Henry's gone now."

"We can't, because I won't play. So there!" answered Beezus. It wasn't as though Henry came over every day to play checkers. He came only once in a while, and then they couldn't play because Ramona was so awful.

Just then the telephone rang and Mother answered it. "Oh, hello, Beatrice," Beezus heard her say. "I was hoping you'd call."

"Tiddlywinks, tiddlywinks, I want to play tiddlywinks," chanted Ramona, shaking her head back and forth.

"Not after the way you spoiled our checker game," said Beezus. "I wouldn't play tiddlywinks with you for a million dollars."

"Yes!" shouted Ramona.

"Children!" Mother put her hand over the mouthpiece of the telephone. "I'm trying to talk to your Aunt Beatrice."

For a moment Beezus forgot her quarrel with Ramona. "Is she coming over today?" she asked eagerly.

"Not today." Mother smiled at Beezus. "But I'll tell her you wish she'd come."

"Tell her she hasn't been here for two whole weeks," said Beezus.

"Tiddlywinks, tiddlywinks," chanted Ramona, more quietly this time. "We're going to play tiddlywinks."

"We are not!" whispered Beezus furiously. And as she looked at Ramona a terrible thought came to her. Right that very instant she was so exasperated with Ramona that she did not like her at all. Not one little bit. Crashing her tricycle into the checkerboard, throwing a tantrum, and shoving a dog into the bathroom—how could one four-year-old be such a pest all in one afternoon? And Ramona wasn't one bit sorry about it, either. She was glad she had driven Henry home with her naughtiness. Just look at her, thought Beezus. Cookie crumbs sticking to the front of her overalls, her hands and face dirty, and those silly paper ears. She's just awful, that's what she is, perfectly awful—and she looks so cheerful. To look at her you wouldn't know she'd done a thing. She's spoiled my whole afternoon and she's happy. She even thinks she'll get me to play tiddlywinks with her. Well, I won't. I won't, because I don't like her *one little bit!*

To get away from Ramona, Beezus stalked into the living room and threw herself into her father's big chair. Not one little

bit, she thought fiercely. But as Beezus sat listening to her mother chatting and laughing over the telephone, she began to feel uncomfortable. She ought to like Ramona. Sisters always liked each other. They were supposed to. Like Mother and Aunt Beatrice. But that was different, Beezus thought quickly. Aunt Beatrice wasn't like Ramona. She was—well, she was Aunt Beatrice, loving and understanding and full of fun. Ramona was noisy and grubby and exasperating.

I feel so mixed up, thought Beezus. Sometimes I don't like Ramona at all, and I'm supposed to like her because she's my sister, and . . . Oh, dear, even if she's little, can't she ever be more like other people's sisters?

4

Ramona and The Apples

"Mother, I'm home," Beezus called, as she burst into the house one afternoon after school.

Mother appeared, wearing her hat and coat and carrying a shopping list in her hand. She kissed Beezus. "How was school today?" she asked.

"All right. We studied about Christopher Columbus," said Beezus.

"Did you, dear?" said Mother absent-mindedly. "I wonder if you'd mind keeping an eye on Ramona for half an hour or so while I do the marketing. She was up so late last night I let her have a long nap this afternoon, and I wasn't able to go out until she woke up."

"All right, I'll look after her," agreed Beezus.

"I told her she could have two marshmallows," said Mother, as she left the house.

Ramona came out of the kitchen with a marshmallow in each hand. Her nose was covered with white powder. "What's Christopher Colummus?" she asked.

"Christopher Columbus," Beezus corrected. "Come here, Ramona. Let me wipe off your nose."

"No," said Ramona, backing away. "I just powdered it." Closing her eyes, Ramona pounded one of the marshmallows against her nose. Powdered sugar flew all over her face. "These are my powder puffs," she explained.

Beezus started to tell Ramona not to be silly, she'd get all sticky, but then decided it would be useless. Ramona never minded being sticky. Instead, she said, "Christopher Columbus is the man who discovered America. He was trying to prove that the world is round."

"Is it?" Ramona sounded puzzled. She beat the other marshmallow against her chin.

"Why, Ramona, don't you know the world is round?" Beezus asked.

Ramona shook her head and powdered her forehead with a marshmallow.

"Well, the world is round just like an orange," Beezus told her. "If you could start out and travel in a perfectly straight line you would come right back where you started from."

"I would?" Ramona looked as if she didn't understand this at all. She also looked as if she didn't care much, because she went right on powdering her face with the marshmallows.

Oh, well, thought Beezus, there's no use trying to explain it to her. She went into the bedroom to change from her school clothes into her play clothes. As usual, she found Ramona's doll, Bendix, lying on her bed, and with a feeling of annoyance she tossed it across the room to Ramona's bed. When she had changed her clothes she went into the kitchen, ate some graham crackers and peanut butter, and helped herself to two marshmallows. If Ramona could have two, it was only fair that she should have two also.

After eating the marshmallows and licking the powdered sugar from her fingers, Beezus decided that reading about Big Steve would be the easiest way to keep Ramona from thinking up some mischief to get into while Mother was away. "Come here, Ramona," she said as she went into the living room. "I'll read to you."

There was no answer. Ramona was not there.

That's funny, thought Beezus, and went into the bedroom. The room was empty. I wonder where she can be, said Beezus to herself. She looked in Mother and Father's room. No one was there. "Ramona!" she called. No answer. "Ramona, where are you?" Still no answer.

Beezus was worried. She did not think Ramona had left the house, because she had not heard any doors open and close. Still, with Ramona you never knew. Maybe she was hiding. Beezus looked under the beds. No Ramona. She looked in the bedroom closets, the hall closet, the linen closet, even the broom closet. Still no Ramona. She ran upstairs to the attic and looked behind the trunks.

Then she ran downstairs to the basement. "Ramona!" she called anxiously, as she peered around in the dim light. The basement was an eerie place with its gray cement walls and the grotesque white arms of the furnace reaching out in all directions. Except for a faint sound from the pilot light everything was silent. Suddenly the furnace lit itself with such a whoosh that Beezus, her heart pounding, turned and ran upstairs. Even though she knew it was only the furnace, she could not help being frightened. The house seemed so empty when no one answered her calls.

Uneasily Beezus sat down in the living room to try to think while she listened to the silence. She must not get panicky. Ramona couldn't be far away. And if she didn't turn up soon, she would telephone the police, the way Mother did the time Ramona got lost because she started out to find the pot of gold at the end of the rainbow.

Thinking of the rainbow reminded Beezus of her attempt to explain to Ramona that the world is round like an orange. Ramona hadn't looked as if she understood, but sometimes it was hard to tell about Ramona. Maybe she just understood the part about coming back where she started from. If Ramona set out to walk to the end of the rainbow, she could easily decide to try walking around the world. That was exactly what she must have done.

The idea frightened Beezus. How would she ever find Ramona? And what would Mother say when she came home and found Ramona gone? To think of Ramona walking in a straight line, hoping to go straight around the world and come back where she started from, trying to cross busy streets alone, honked at by trucks, barked at by strange dogs, tired, hungry... But I can't just sit here, thought Beezus. I've got to do something. I'll run out and look up and down the street. She can't have gone far.

At that moment Beezus heard a noise. She thought it came from the basement, but she was not certain. Tiptoeing to the cold-air intake in the hall, she bent over and listened. Sure enough, a noise so faint she could scarcely hear it came up through the furnace pipe. So the house wasn't empty after all! Just wait until she got hold of Ramona!

Beezus snapped on the basement light and ran down the steps. "Ramona, come out," she ordered. "I know you're here."

The only answer was a chomping sound from the corner of the basement. Beezus ran around the furnace and there, in the dimly lit corner, sat Ramona, eating an apple.

Beezus was so relieved to see Ramona safe, and at the same time so angry with her for hiding, that she couldn't say anything. She just stood there filled with the exasperated mixed-up feeling that Ramona so often gave her.

"Hello," said Ramona through a bite of apple.

"Ramona Geraldine Quimby!" exclaimed Beezus, when she had found her voice. "What do you think you're doing?"

"Playing hide-and-seek," answered Ramona.

"Well, I'm not!" snapped Beezus. "It takes two to play hide-and-seek."

"You found me," Ramona pointed out.

"Oh . . ." Once again Beezus couldn't find any words. To think she had worried so, when all the time Ramona was sitting in the basement listening to her call. And eating an apple, too!

As she stood in front of Ramona, Beezus's eyes began to grow accustomed to the dim light and she realized what Ramona was doing. She stared, horrified at what she saw. As if hiding were not enough! What would Mother say when she came home and found what Ramona had been up to this time?

Ramona was sitting on the floor beside a box of apples. Lying around her on the cement floor were a number of apples— each with one bite out of it. While Beezus stared, Ramona reached into the box, selected an apple, took one big bite out of the reddest part, and tossed the rest of the apple onto the floor. While she noisily chewed that bite, she reached into the apple box again.

"Ramona!" cried Beezus, horrified. "You can't do that."

"I can, too," said Ramona through her mouthful.

"Stop it," ordered Beezus. "Stop it this instant! You can't eat one bite and then throw the rest away."

"But the first bite tastes best," explained Ramona reasonably, as she reached into the box again.

Beezus had to admit that Ramona was right. The first bite of an apple always did taste best. Ramona's sharp little teeth were about to sink into another apple when Beezus snatched it from her.

"That's my apple," screamed Ramona.

"It is not!" said Beezus angrily, stamping her foot. "One apple is all you're supposed to have. Just wait till Mother finds out!"

Ramona stopped screaming and watched Beezus. Then, seeing how angry Beezus was, she smiled and offered her an apple. "I want to share the apples," she said sweetly.

"Oh, no, you don't," said Beezus. "And don't try to work that sharing business on me!" That was one of the difficult things about Ramona. When she had done something wrong, she often tried to get out of it by offering to share something. She heard a lot about sharing at nursery school.

Now what am I going to do, Beezus wondered. I promised Mother I would keep an eye on Ramona, and look what she's gone and done. How am I going to explain this to Mother? I'll get scolded too. And all the apples. What can we do with them?

Beezus was sure about one thing. She no longer felt mixed up about Ramona. Ramona was perfectly impossible. She snatched Ramona's hand. "You come upstairs with me and be good until Mother gets back," she ordered, pulling her sister up the basement stairs.

Ramona broke away from her and ran into the living room. She climbed onto a chair, where she sat with her legs sticking straight out in front of her. She folded her hands in her lap and said in a little voice, "Don't bother me. This is my quiet time. I'm supposed to be resting."

Quiet times were something else Ramona had learned about at nursery school. When she didn't want to do something, she often insisted she was supposed to be having a

quiet time. Beezus was about to say that Ramona didn't need a quiet time, because she hadn't been playing hard and Mother had said she had already had a nap, but then she thought better of it. If Ramona wanted to sit in a chair and be quiet, let her. She might stay out of mischief until Mother came home.

Beezus had no sooner sat down to work on her pot holders, planning to keep an eye on Ramona at the same time, when the telephone rang. It must be Aunt Beatrice, she thought, before she answered. Mother and Aunt Beatrice almost always talked to each other about this time of day.

"Hello, darling, how are you?" asked Aunt Beatrice.

"Oh, Aunt Beatrice," cried Beezus, "Ramona has just done something awful, and I was supposed to be looking after her. I don't know what to do." She told about Ramona's hiding in the cellar and biting into half a box of apples.

Aunt Beatrice laughed. "Leave it to Ramona to think up something new," she said. "Do you know what I'd do if I were you?"

"What?" asked Beezus eagerly, already feeling better because she had confided her troubles to her aunt.

"I wouldn't say anything more about it," said Aunt Beatrice. "Lots of times little children are naughty because they want to attract attention. I have an idea that saying nothing about her naughtiness will worry Ramona more than a scolding."

Beezus thought this over and decided her aunt was right. If there was one thing Ramona couldn't stand, it was being ignored. "I'll try it," she said.

"And about the apples," Aunt Beatrice went on. "All I can suggest is that your mother might make applesauce."

This struck Beezus as being funny, and as she and her aunt laughed together over the telephone she felt much better.

"Tell your mother I phoned," said Aunt Beatrice.

"I will," promised Beezus. "And please come over soon."

When Beezus heard her mother drive up, she rushed out to meet her and tell her the story of what Ramona had done. She also told her Aunt Beatrice's suggestion.

"Oh, dear, leave it to Ramona," sighed Mother. "Your aunt is right. We won't say a word about it."

Beezus helped her mother carry the groceries into the house. Ramona came into the kitchen to see if there were any animal crackers among the packages. She waited a few minutes for her sister to tattle on her. Then, when Beezus did not say anything, she announced, "I was bad this afternoon." She sounded pleased with herself.

"Were you?" remarked Mother calmly. "Beezus, I think applesauce would be good for dessert tonight. Will you run down and bring up some apples?"

When Ramona looked disappointed at having failed to arouse any interest, Beezus and her mother exchanged smiles. "I want to help," said Ramona, rather than be left out.

Beezus and Ramona made four trips to

the basement to bring up all the bitten apples. Mother said nothing about their appearance, but spent the rest of the afternoon peeling and cooking apples. After she had finished, she filled her two largest mixing bowls, a casserole, and the bowl of her electric mixer with applesauce. It took her quite a while to rearrange the contents of the refrigerator to make room for all the applesauce.

When Beezus saw her father coming home she ran out on the front walk to tell him what had happened. He, too, agreed that Aunt Beatrice's suggestion was a good one.

"Daddy!" shrieked Ramona when her father came in.

"How's my girl?" asked Father as he picked Ramona up and kissed her.

"Oh, I was bad today," said Ramona.

"Were you?" said Father as he put her down. "Was there any mail today?"

Ramona looked crestfallen. "I was very bad," she persisted. "I was awful."

Father sat down and picked up the evening paper.

"I hid from Beezus and I bit lots and lots of apples," Ramona went on insistently.

"Mmm," remarked Father from behind the paper. "I see they're going to raise bus fares again."

"Lots and lots of apples," repeated Ramona in a loud voice.

"They raised bus fares last year," Father went on, winking at Beezus from behind the paper. "The public isn't going to stand for this."

Ramona looked puzzled and then disappointed, but she did not say anything.

Father dropped his paper. "Something certainly smells good," he said. "It smells like applesauce. I hope so. There's nothing I like better than a big dish of applesauce for dessert."

Because Mother had been so busy making applesauce, dinner was a little late that night. At the table Ramona was unusually well behaved. She did not interrupt and she did not try to share her carrots, the way she usually did because she did not like carrots.

As Beezus cleared the table and Mother served dessert—which was fig Newtons and, of course, applesauce—Ramona's good behavior continued. Beezus found she was not very hungry for applesauce, but the rest of the family appeared to enjoy it. After Beezus had wiped the dishes for Mother she sat down to embroider her pot holders. She had decided to give Aunt Beatrice the pot holder with the dancing knife and fork on it instead of the one with the laughing teakettle.

Ramona approached her with *Big Steve the Steam Shovel* in her hand. "Beezus, will you read to me?" she asked.

She thinks I'll say no and then she can make a fuss, thought Beezus. Well, I won't give her a chance. "All right," she said, putting down her pot holder and taking the book, while Ramona climbed into the chair beside her.

"Big Steve was a steam shovel. He was the biggest steam shovel in the whole city," Beezus read. "'Gr-r-r,' growled Big Steve when he moved the earth to make way for the new highway."

Father dropped his newspaper and looked at his two daughters sitting side by side. "I wonder," he said, "exactly how long this is going to last."

"Just enjoy it while it does," said Mother, who was basting patches on the knees of a pair of Ramona's overalls.

"Gr-r-r," growled Ramona. "Gr-r-r."

Beezus also wondered just how long this would go on. She didn't enjoy growling like a steam shovel and she felt that perhaps Ramona was getting her own way after all. I'm trying to like her like I'm supposed to, anyhow, Beezus thought, and I do like her more than I did this afternoon when I found her in the basement. But what on earth will Mother ever do with all that applesauce?

5
A Party at The Quimbys'

Saturday morning turned out to be cold and rainy. Beezus wiped the breakfast dishes for her mother and listened to Ramona, who was riding her tricycle around the house, singing, "Copycat, cappycot, copycat, cappycot," over and over at the top of her voice, because she liked the sound of the words.

Beezus and her mother finished the

dishes and went into the bedroom to put clean sheets on the beds. "Copycat, cappy-cot," droned Ramona's singsong.

"Ramona, why don't you sing something else?" Mother asked at last. "We've been listening to that for a long time."

"O.K.," agreed Ramona. "I'm going to have a par-tee," she sang. "I'm going to have a par-tee."

"Thank you, Ramona. That's better." Mother held one end of a pillow under her chin while she slipped the other end into a fresh case. "You know, that reminds me," she said to Beezus. "What would you like to do to celebrate your birthday next week?"

Beezus thought a minute. "Well . . . I'd like to have Aunt Beatrice over for dinner. She hasn't been here for such a long time. And I'd like to have a birthday cake with pink frosting." Beezus smoothed a fresh sheet over the bed. She almost enjoyed helping Mother when they could talk without Ramona's interrupting all the time. The rain beating on the windows and Ramona's happy singsong made the day seem cozy and peaceful.

"All right, that's exactly what we'll do." Mother seemed really pleased with Beezus's suggestions. "It's a long time since we've seen Aunt Beatrice, but of course teachers always have a lot to do when school starts." Beezus noticed that Mother gave a little sigh as she smoothed her side of the sheet. "She'll probably have more time now that the semester has started and it really isn't long before Thanksgiving and Christmas vacations. We'll see a lot of her then."

Why, Mother misses Aunt Beatrice too, thought Beezus. I believe she misses her as much as I do, even though she never says so.

Leaving Beezus with the new and surprising thought that grown-ups sometimes missed each other, Mother gathered up the sheets and pillowcases that had been removed from the beds and carried them to the basement. While she was downstairs the telephone rang. "Answer it, will you, Beezus," Mother called.

When Beezus picked up the telephone, a hurried voice said, "This is Mrs. Kemp. Do you mind if I leave Willa Jean when I bring Howie over this afternoon?"

"Just a minute. I'll ask Mother." Beezus called down the basement stairs, repeating the question.

"Why, no, I guess not," Mother replied.

"Mother says it's all right," Beezus said into the telephone.

"Thank you," said Mrs. Kemp. "Now I'll (Howie, stop banging!) have a chance to do some shopping."

Well, thought Beezus when she had hung up, things won't be quiet around here much longer. Howie, who was in Ramona's class at nursery school, was the noisiest little boy she knew, and he and Ramona often quarreled. Willa Jean was at the awkward age—too big to be a baby and not big enough to be out of diapers.

"You know," said Mother, when she came up from the basement, "I don't remember telling Mrs. Kemp that Howie could come over this afternoon, but maybe I did. I've had so much on my mind lately, trying to get the nursery-school rummage sale organized."

After an early lunch Mother decided there would be enough time to wash everybody's hair before Howie and Willa Jean arrived. She put on her oldest dress, because Ramona always squirmed and got soap all over her. Then she stood Ramona on a chair, made her lean over the kitchen sink, and went to work. Ramona howled, as she always did when her hair was washed. When

Mother finished she rubbed Ramona's hair with a bath towel, turned up the furnace thermostat so the house would be extra-warm, and gave Ramona two graham crackers to make up for the indignity of having her hair washed.

Then Beezus stepped onto the stool and bent over the sink for her turn. After Mother had washed her own hair and before she went into the bathroom to put it up in pin curls, she said to Beezus, "Would you mind getting out the vacuum cleaner and picking up those graham-cracker crumbs Ramona spilled on the rug?"

Beezus did not mind. She rather liked running the vacuum cleaner if her mother didn't make a regular chore of it.

"I'm going to have a par-tee," sang Ramona above the roar of the vacuum cleaner. Then she changed her song. "Here comes my par-tee!" she chanted.

Beezus glanced out the window and quickly switched off the vacuum cleaner. Four small children were coming up the front walk through the rain. A car stopped in front of the house and three children climbed out. Two more were splashing across the street.

"Mother!" cried Beezus. "Come here, quick. Ramona wasn't pretending!"

Mother appeared in the living room just as the doorbell rang. One side of her hair was up in pin curls and the other side hung wet and dripping on the towel around her neck. "Oh, my goodness!" she exclaimed when she understood the situation. "That explains Mrs. Kemp's phone call. Ramona, how could you?"

"I wanted to have a party," explained Ramona. "I invited everybody yesterday."

The doorbell rang again, this time long and hard. There was the sound of many rubber boots jumping up and down on the porch.

"Mother, we just can't have a party with our hair wet," wailed Beezus.

"What else can we do?" Mother sounded desperate. "They're here and we can't very well send them home. Their mothers have probably planned to shop or something while we look after them."

Ramona struggled with the doorknob and managed to open the heavy front door. Mrs. Kemp stopped her car in front of the Quimbys', and Howie and Willa Jean hopped out. "I'll pick them up at four," she called gaily. "I'm so glad to have a chance to get out and do some shopping."

Mother smiled weakly and looked at all the children on the porch.

"Where do you suppose she found them all?" whispered Beezus. "I don't even know some of them."

"All right, children." Mother spoke firmly. "Leave your wet boots and raincoats on the porch."

"I've got a par-tee," sang Ramona happily.

Beezus, who had plenty of experience with Ramona and her boots, knew where she was needed. She started pulling off boots and unbuttoning raincoats.

"What on earth shall we do with them on a day like this?" whispered Mother.

Beezus grabbed a muddy boot. "Hold still," she said firmly to its owner. "They'll expect refreshments," she said.

"I know," sighed Mother. "You'll have to put on your coat and run down to the market— Oh, no, you can't go out in this rain with your hair wet." Mother tugged at another boot. "I'll have to see what I can find in the kitchen."

Beezus and her mother herded the wiggling, squealing crowd into the front bedroom and went to work removing sweaters, jackets, caps, and mittens. In between Beezus pulled three children out of the closet, dragged one out from under the bed, and snatched her mother's bottle of best perfume from another.

"All right, everybody out of here," Beezus ordered, when the last mitten was removed and her mother had hurried into the kitchen. "We'll go into the living room and . . . and do something," she finished lamely. "Ramona, bring some of your toys out of your room."

"Bingle-bongle-by!" shouted Howie, just to make some noise.

"Bingle-bongle-by!" The others joined in with great delight. It was such a nice noisy thing to yell. "Bingle-bongle-by," they screamed at the tops of their voices as they scampered into the living room. "Bingle-bongle-by."

Howie grabbed the vacuum cleaner, turned on the switch, and charged across the room. "I'll suck you up!" he shouted. "I'll suck everybody up in the vacuum cleaner!"

"Bingle-bongle-by!" shouted the others above the roar of the vacuum cleaner.

One little girl began to cry. "I don't want to be sucked up in the vacuum cleaner," she sobbed. Willa Jean, looking bulgy because of the diapers and plastic pants under her overalls, clung to a chair and wept.

Ramona appeared with her arms full of toys, but no one paid any attention to them. The vacuum cleaner was much more fun.

"I want to push the vacuum cleaner," screamed Susan, who lived in the next block.

Ramona offered Susan her panda bear, but Susan did not want it. Ramona hit Susan with the panda. "You take my bear," she ordered. "This is my party and you're supposed to do what I say."

"I don't want your old bear," answered Susan.

Beezus tried to grab the vacuum cleaner, but Howie was too quick for her. The room was getting uncomfortably hot, so Beezus darted to the thermostat to turn down the heat. Then she dashed to the other side of the room and disconnected the vacuum cleaner at the wall. It died with a noisy groan. Suddenly everyone was quiet, waiting to see what would happen.

"Hey," protested Howie, "you can't do that."

Beezus frantically tried to think of some way to keep fifteen small children busy and out of mischief. At least, she thought there were fifteen. They didn't stand still long enough to be counted.

"Where's the party?" one little boy asked.

Ramona appeared with more toys, which she dumped on the floor. This time she brought a drum. Howie quickly lost interest in the vacuum cleaner and grabbed the drum. Beezus seized the vacuum cleaner and shoved it into the hall closet, while Howie began to beat the drum. "I'm leading a parade," he said.

"You are not," contradicted Ramona. "This is my party."

Susan snatched a pink plastic horn and tooted it. "I'm in the parade too," she said.

"I want to be in the parade! I want to be

in the parade!" cried the others.

That was it! They could play parade! Beezus ran to the bedroom and found a whistle and a couple of horns left over from a Halloween party. What else could be used in a parade? Flags, of course! But what could she use for flags? Beezus thought fast. She gathered up two yardsticks and several rulers; then she ran to the front bedroom and snatched some of her father's handkerchiefs from a drawer. She had to move fast before the children grew tired of the idea.

"I want to be in the parade!" screamed the children.

"Mother, help me," cried Beezus.

Somehow Beezus and her mother got Father's handkerchiefs tied to the sticks and distributed to the children who did not have noisemakers.

Howie banged the drum. "Follow me," he ordered, beginning to march. The others followed, blowing whistles, tooting horns, waving flags.

"No!" screamed Ramona, who wanted to boss her own party.

"You wanted a party," Mother reminded her. "If your guests want to play parade, you'd better join them."

Ramona scowled, but she took a flag and joined the parade rather than be left out entirely at her own party.

"Playing parade was a wonderful idea." Mother smiled at Beezus. "I hope it lasts."

"So do I," Beezus agreed.

"Bingle-bongle-by," yelled the flag wavers.

Howie led the parade, including a sulky Ramona, out of the living room, down the hall, through the kitchen and dining room, and back into the living room again. Willa Jean toddled along at the end of the procession. Beezus was afraid the parade might

break up, but all the children appeared delighted with the game. Into the bedroom they marched and out again. Beezus opened the basement door. Down the steps Howie led the parade. Willa Jean had to go down the steps backwards on her hands and knees. Three times around the furnace marched the parade and up the steps again before Willa Jean was halfway down.

Beezus opened the door to the attic. Up

the steps marched the parade. Stamp, stamp, stamp went their feet overhead. Stamp, stamp, stamp.

Beezus remembered something Ramona had enjoyed when she was still in diapers. She lugged Willa Jean up the basement steps, sat her in the middle of the kitchen floor, and handed her the egg beater. "There. Don't step on her," she said to her mother.

"Thank goodness," sighed Mother. "Maybe they'll play parade long enough for us to fix something for them to eat."

"What'll we give them?" Beezus asked.

Mother laughed. "This is a wonderful chance to get rid of all that applesauce. Let's hurry and get it ready before they get tired of their game. Get the colored paper napkins out of the cupboard and—oh, dear, what shall we do for chairs?"

"They can sit on the floor," suggested

Beezus, looking through the cupboard for napkins.

"I guess they'll have to." Mother took the applesauce out of the refrigerator. "If we put a couple of sheets down for them to sit on, maybe they won't get applesauce on the rug."

The parade tramped down the attic stairs and through the kitchen. "But Mother," said Beezus, when the drum and horns had disappeared into the basement again, "the only napkins I can find are for St. Valentine's Day and Halloween. They won't do."

"They'll have to do," said Mother.

Beezus spread two sheets in the middle of the living-room floor. Then she went into the kitchen to help Mother, who was tearing open three boxes of fig Newtons. "It's a good thing I bought these at that sale last week," she remarked.

"Are we going to give them lemonade or

anything to drink?" Beezus asked.

"Not on my living-room rug." Mother rapidly spooned applesauce into dishes. "Applesauce and fig Newtons are bad enough."

"Maybe if we feed them right away some of them will think the party is over and go home." Beezus piled fig Newtons on two plates.

"I hope so. This many small children in the house on a rainy day is too much." The parade stamped across the attic floor again, and Mother had to raise her voice to make herself heard. "It sounds as if they were coming through the ceiling."

"Let's catch them the next time they come through the kitchen and hand out the applesauce," Beezus shouted back. "Then maybe we can get them to march into the living room."

It was not long before Howie led the

parade into the kitchen again. He stopped so suddenly that the children bumped into one another. "When do we eat?" he demanded.

"Now." Beezus thrust a dish of apple-sauce and a spoon into his hands.

"I want some," cried the others.

Mother handed a second child some applesauce. "Forward march!" she ordered.

Beezus led Howie into the living room, and the rest of the parade followed with their applesauce. "You sit there," she said to Howie, pointing to a place on the sheet. She was relieved to see the others seat them-selves around the edge of the sheet. Quickly she handed around paper napkins.

"I want one with witches on it," demanded a boy who had a Valentine napkin.

"I want one with hearts on it," wailed a girl who had a Halloween napkin.

Beezus hastily counted the napkins. Yes, there were enough of each kind to go around. Two napkins apiece would be safer anyway. She handed each child a second napkin and they all began to eat their applesauce, except one little girl who didn't like applesauce. Ramona was beaming, because refreshments were the most important part of any party and now at last her guests were behaving the way she wanted them to.

Mother came out of the kitchen with the plates of fig Newtons, which she handed to Beezus. "Here, pass these around," she said. "I think I'd better help Willa Jean." Willa Jean knew how to eat with a spoon. The trouble was, she had to pick up the food with her left hand and put it into the spoon, which she held in her right hand. Then, most of the time, she was able to get it into her mouth.

Ramona, her face shining with happiness, looked at her friends sharing the applesauce. "Those cookies are filled with worms.

Chopped-up worms!" she gleefully told everyone.

"Why, Ramona!" Beezus was shocked. "They aren't either. They're filled with ground-up figs. You know that."

Ramona did not answer. Her mouth was full of fig Newtons.

Beezus passed the plate to a boy named Joey. "I don't like worms," he said.

"I don't like worms," said the next little girl, who had applesauce all over her chin.

Beezus noticed that Ramona was beginning to scowl. When Howie refused a cookie, it was too much for Ramona. "You eat that!" she shouted.

"I won't," yelled Howie. "You can't make me."

Ramona jumped up, spilling her applesauce on the sheet. She thrust a nibbled fig Newton at Howie. "You eat that," she repeated as she stepped into the applesauce.

"It's my party and I want you to eat it!"

Howie knocked the cookie out of her hand. Ramona grabbed a handful of fig Newtons and thrust them at Susan. "Eat these," she shouted.

Susan began to cry. "They're full of

worms," she sobbed. "I don't like worms."

"They're *pretend* worms," yelled Ramona.

"No, they're not," cried Susan. "They're real!"

"You eat these," Ramona yelled, thrusting her handful of cookies at the children, who backed away. Ramona stamped her feet and screamed. Then she threw the fig Newtons at her guests as hard as she could.

"My mother won't let me eat worms!" shouted a little boy.

Ramona threw herself on the floor and kicked.

"Ramona, stop that!" Mother appeared from the kitchen with Willa Jean balanced on one hip. She grabbed Ramona by one arm and tried to drag her to her feet, but Ramona's legs were like rubber.

"All right, Howie, forward march!" Beezus ordered, hoping to draw attention from Ramona. No one moved. It was much more fun to see what was going to happen to Ramona.

"This is my party! They're supposed to eat the refreshments!" Ramona howled, banging her heels on the floor.

"Ramona, you're acting like a two-year-old. You may go to your room and close the door until you can behave yourself," said Mother quietly.

Ramona kicked harder to show that she was not going to mind unless she felt like it.

"Ramona," said Mother even more quietly. "Don't make me count to ten."

Gasping with sobs, Ramona got up from the floor and ran into the bedroom, where she slammed the door as hard as she could.

"All right, parade," said Mother wearily. "Forward march."

Up and down, whistling, banging, tooting, marched the parade. Mother sat Willa Jean down and was just beginning to gather up the dishes and sheets when a car stopped in front of the house and Mrs. Kemp got out. "At last," sighed Mother, hurrying to the door.

"I've come for Howie and Willa Jean," said Mrs. Kemp, as several other cars stopped in front of the Quimbys'. The parade marched into the living room.

"I don't want to go home," protested Howie, when he saw his mother.

"The party must have been a success," Mrs. Kemp observed.

"It certainly was." Mother tried to push the uncurled side of her hair behind her ear and to smooth out her rumpled old dress.

"I like to play parade," said Howie, "but I didn't like what they had to eat."

"Why, Howie," scolded Mrs. Kemp. "We must remember our manners."

Ramona, her face streaked with tears, came out of her room and stood staring unhappily at her departing guests. When the last child had struggled into his boots, she looked tearfully at her mother. "I'm behaving myself now," she said meekly.

Mother dropped wearily into a chair. "Ramona, if you wanted a party, why didn't you ask me to have one?"

"Because when I ask you don't let me do things," explained Ramona, sniffing.

Beezus couldn't help feeling there was some truth in Ramona's remark. She had often felt that way herself, especially when she was younger. "Mother, did I do things like Ramona when I was four?" she asked.

"You did some of the things Ramona does now," said Mother thoughtfully, "but you were really very different. You were quieter, for one thing."

This pleased Beezus. One of the reasons she sometimes disliked Ramona was that she was never quiet when she could manage to be noisy.

"Of course there are some things that all four-year-olds do," Mother continued, "but even sisters are usually different. Just the way your Aunt Beatrice and I were different when we were girls. I was a bookworm and went to the library two or three times a week. She was the best hopscotch player and the fastest rope jumper in the neighborhood. And she was better at jacks than anybody in our whole school."

This surprised Beezus. She had never thought about her mother and aunt as children before. She tried to picture her schoolteacher aunt jumping rope and found to her surprise that it was not very hard to do. Of course Mother and Aunt Beatrice must have been different when they were girls, because they were so different now that they were grown up. And she was glad they were different. She loved them both.

"Did I have tantrums, too?" Beezus asked.

"Once in a while," said Mother. "I always dreaded cutting your fingernails, because you kicked and screamed."

Beezus could not help feeling silly. Imagine having a tantrum over a little thing like having her fingernails cut!

Then Ramona spoke up. "I don't cry when you cut my fingernails," she boasted.

"Yes, but you scream when you have your hair washed," Beezus could not help reminding her.

"Ramona," said Mother, "you were a very naughty girl this afternoon. What are we going to do with you?"

Ramona stopped sniffing and looked interested. "Lock me in a closet for a million years?" she suggested cheerfully.

Mother and Beezus exchanged glances. How quickly Ramona recovered!

"Make me sleep outdoors in the rain?" Obviously Ramona was enjoying herself.

"Not let me have anything to eat but carrots?"

Mother laughed and looked at Beezus. "I'm afraid all we can do is wait for her to grow up," she said.

And when Mother said *we* like that, Beezus almost felt sorry for Ramona, because she would have to wait such a long time to be grown up.

6

Beezus's Birthday

When Beezus came home from school on the afternoon of her tenth birthday, she felt that so far the day had been perfect—packages by her plate at breakfast, a new dress to wear to school, the whole class singing "Happy Birthday" just for her. But the best part was still to come. Aunt Beatrice was coming for dinner.

Beezus could hardly wait to tell her aunt

about acting the part of Sacajawea leading Lewis and Clark across the plains to Oregon at a P.T.A. meeting. And of course Aunt Beatrice would bring more presents—very special presents, because she was Aunt Beatrice's namesake. And at dinner there would be a beautiful birthday cake with ten candles. Mother had probably worked all afternoon baking and decorating the cake and now had it hidden away in a cupboard.

When Mother kissed Beezus she had said, "I'm sorry, Beezus, but I'll have to ask you to keep Ramona out of the kitchen for a while."

"Why?" asked Beezus, thinking her mother was planning a surprise.

"So I can bake your birthday cake," Mother explained.

"Isn't it baked yet?" exclaimed Beezus. "Oh, Mother."

"This has been one of those days when I

couldn't seem to get anything done," said Mother. "It was my morning for the nursery-school car pool. After I picked up all the children and drove them to nursery school and came home and did the breakfast dishes and made the beds, it was time to pick up the children and take them all home again. And after lunch I started the cake and had just creamed the sugar and butter in the electric mixer when I was called to the telephone. When I came back, what do you think had happened?"

"What?" asked Beezus, pretty sure Ramona had something to do with it.

"Ramona had dropped all the eggs in the house into the batter and had started the mixer," said Mother.

"Shells and all?" asked Beezus, horrified.

"Shells and all," repeated Mother wearily. "And so I had to get out the car again and drive to the market and buy more eggs."

"Ramona, what did you have to go and do a thing like that for?" Beezus demanded of her little sister, who was playing with her doll Bendix.

"To see what would happen," answered Ramona.

She doesn't look a bit sorry, thought Beezus crossly. Spoiling my birthday cake like that!

"Don't worry, dear. There's still plenty of

time to bake another," said Mother. "If you'll just keep Ramona out of the kitchen, I can get it into the oven in no time at all."

That made Beezus feel better. At least she would have a birthday cake, even if it did mean looking after Ramona for a while.

"Read to me," Ramona demanded. "Read about Big Steve."

"I'll read to you, but I won't read that book," said Beezus, going to the bookcase. She really wanted to read one of her birthday books, called *202 Things to Do on a Rainy Afternoon*, but she knew Ramona would insist on a story. "How about Hänsel and Gretel?" she asked. Next to stories with lots of noise, Ramona liked stories about witches, goblins, or ogres.

"Yes, I like Hänsel and Gretel," agreed Ramona, as she climbed on the davenport and sat Bendix beside her. "O.K., I'm ready. Now you can begin."

Beezus curled up at the other end of the davenport with *Grimm's Fairy Tales.* "Once upon a time . . ." she began, and Ramona listened contentedly. When she did not have to make noises like machinery Beezus enjoyed reading to Ramona, and this afternoon reading aloud was particularly pleasant, with Mother in the kitchen baking a birthday cake. As Beezus read she listened to the whir of the mixer and the sound of eggs being cracked against a bowl.

Beezus read about Hänsel's leaving a trail of crumbs behind him as he and Gretel went into the woods. She read the part Ramona liked best, about the witch's trying to fatten Hänsel. Ramona listened wide-eyed until Beezus came to the end of the story, where Gretel pushed the witch into the oven and escaped through the woods with her brother.

"That's a good story," said Ramona, as she

jumped down from the davenport.

Surprised that Ramona didn't demand another story, Beezus picked up *202 Things to Do on a Rainy Afternoon* and began to read. She was learning how to make a necklace out of beans and pumpkin seeds painted with fingernail polish when a lovely sweet vanilla fragrance began to fill the house, and Beezus knew her birthday cake was safely in the oven at last.

Ramona's unusual silence made Beezus glance up from her book. "Ramona!" she cried, when she saw what her little sister was doing. "Stop that right away!"

Ramona was busy pulling graham-cracker crumbs out of the pocket of her overalls and sprinkling them across the rug. "I'm Hänsel leaving a trail of crumbs through the woods," she said, digging more crumbs out of her pocket. "My father is a poor woodcutter."

"Oh, Ramona," said Beezus, but she had to giggle at the picture of Father as a poor woodcutter.

Ramona sprinkled more crumbs on the rug, and Beezus knew she had to do something about it. "Why don't you pretend you're Gretel?" she suggested, because Gretel would not leave crumbs on the rug.

"O.K.," agreed Ramona.

That was easy, thought Beezus, and went on reading about making a complete set of doll furniture out of old milk cartons. How good her birthday cake smelled! She hoped Mother would remember she had asked for pink frosting. She heard the oven door open and close. Mother must be peeking into the oven to see how my cake is coming along, she thought.

Beezus read on, absorbed in the directions for making a vase out of an old tomato-juice can. Something smells funny, she thought as she turned a page. Then she stopped and sniffed. The air was no longer filled with the lovely warm fragrance of a baking cake. It was filled with a horrid rubbery smell. That's funny, thought Beezus. I wonder what it can be. She sniffed again. Maybe somebody was burning trash outside and the smell was coming in through the window.

Mother came into the living room from the bedroom. "Beezus, do you smell something rubbery?" she asked anxiously.

"Yes, and it smells awful," said Beezus. Ramona held her nose.

Mother sniffed again. "It smells as if something is scorching, too."

Beezus went into the kitchen, where she found the smell so strong that it made her cough. "It's worse in here, Mother," she called, as she looked to see if anything was burning on the stove. Then Beezus remembered the oven. "Mother," she said in a worried voice, "you don't suppose something has happened to my birthday cake again?"

"Of course not," said Mother, coming into the kitchen and opening the window. "What could happen to it?"

Just to be sure, Beezus cautiously opened the oven door. "Mother!" she cried, horrified at what she saw. "Look!" Ramona's rubber doll, Bendix, leaned over the edge of the cake pan, her head and arms buried in the batter. Her dress was scorched to a golden tan. "Oh, Mother!" repeated Beezus. Her birthday cake, her beautiful, fragrant birthday cake, was ruined.

"Is the witch done yet?" Ramona asked.

"Ramona—" began Mother and stopped. She couldn't think of anything to say. Silently she turned off the oven and, with a pot holder, pulled out the doll and the remains of the cake.

"Ramona Geraldine Quimby!" said Beezus angrily. "You're just awful, that's what you are! Just plain awful. Spoiling your own sister's birthday cake!"

"You told me to pretend I was Gretel," protested Ramona. "And Gretel pushed the witch into the oven."

Beezus looked at the cake and burst into tears.

Ramona promptly began to cry too. This made Beezus even angrier. "You stop crying," she ordered Ramona furiously. "It was my birthday cake and I'm the one that's supposed to be crying."

"Girls!" said Mother in a tired voice. "Ramona, you have been very naughty. You know better than to put anything into the oven. Now go to your room and stay there until I say you can come out."

Sniffling, Ramona started toward the bedroom.

"And don't you dare put your toys on my bed," said Beezus. "Mother, can you fix the cake?"

"I'm afraid not." Mother poked at the cake with her finger. "It's fallen, and anyway it would probably taste like burnt rubber."

Beezus tried to brush the tears out of her eyes. "Ramona always spoils everything. Now I won't have any birthday cake, and Aunt Beatrice is coming and it won't be like a birthday at all."

"I know Ramona is a problem but we'll just have to be patient, because she's little," said Mother, as she scraped the cake into the garbage can. "And you will still have a cake. I'll phone your Aunt Beatrice and have her bring one from the bakery."

"Oh, Mother, will you?" asked Beezus.

"That's what I'll do," said Mother. "Now run along and wash your face and you'll feel better."

But as Beezus held her face cloth under the faucet she was not at all sure she would feel better. For Ramona to spoil one birthday cake was bad enough, but *two* . . . Probably nobody else in the whole world had a little sister who had spoiled two birthday cakes on the same day.

Beezus scrubbed away the tear stains, feeling more and more sorry for herself for having such a little sister. If Ramona were only bigger, things might be different; but since she was so much younger, she would always be . . . well, a pest. Then the terrible thought came to Beezus again—the thought she had had the time Ramona bit into all the apples and the time she shoved the dog into the bathroom. She tried not to think the thought, but she couldn't help it. There were times when she did not love Ramona. This was one of them. Everyone knew sisters were supposed to love each other. Look how much Mother and Aunt Beatrice loved each other. Beezus felt very gloomy indeed as she dried her face. She was a terrible girl who did not love her little sister. Like a wicked sister in a fairy tale. And on her birthday, too, a day that was supposed to be happy.

When Beezus went into the living room, Mother switched off the vacuum cleaner, which had been sucking up the crumbs Ramona had sprinkled on the rug. "Aunt Beatrice said she would be delighted to bring a cake. She knows a bakery that makes very special birthday cakes," she said, smiling at Beezus. "You mustn't let Ramona spoil your birthday."

Beezus felt a little better. She curled up on the davenport again with *202 Things to Do on a Rainy Afternoon* and read about making Christmas tree ornaments out of cellophane straws, until she heard her aunt's car turn into the driveway. Then she flung her book aside and ran out to greet her.

"Happy birthday, darling!" cried Aunt Beatrice, as she set the brake and opened the door of her yellow convertible.

Joyfully Beezus ran over to the car and kissed her aunt. "Did you bring the cake?" she asked.

"I certainly did," answered Aunt Beatrice. "The best birthday cake I could find. And that isn't all I brought. Here, help me carry these packages while I carry the cake. We mustn't let anything happen to *this* cake!"

And the way Aunt Beatrice laughed made Beezus laugh too. Her aunt gave her three packages, two large and one small, to carry.

"The little package is for Ramona," explained Aunt Beatrice. "So she won't feel left out."

Mother came out of the house and hugged her sister. "Hello, Bea," she said. "I'm so glad you could come. What would I ever do without you?"

"It's good to see you, Dorothy," answered Aunt Beatrice. "And what's an aunt for if she can't come to the rescue with a birthday cake once in a while?"

As Beezus watched her mother and her

aunt, arm in arm, go into the house, she thought how different they were—Mother so tall and comfortable-looking and Aunt Beatrice so small and gay—and yet how happy they looked together. Smiling, Beezus carried the gifts into the house. Aunt Beatrice always brought such beautiful packages, wrapped in fancy paper and tied with big, fluffy bows.

Aunt Beatrice handed the cake box to Mother. "Be sure you put it in a safe place," she said, and laughed again.

"May I open the packages now?" Beezus asked eagerly, although she felt it was almost too bad to untie such beautiful bows.

"Of course you may," answered Aunt Beatrice.

"Where's Ramona?"

A subdued Ramona came out of the bedroom to receive her present. She tore off the wrapping, but Beezus painstakingly untied the ribbon on one of her presents and removed the paper carefully so she wouldn't tear it. Her new book, *202 Things to Do on a Rainy Afternoon*, suggested pasting pretty paper on a gallon ice-cream carton to make a wastebasket.

"Oh, Aunt Beatrice," exclaimed Beezus, as she opened her first package. It was a real grown-up sewing box. It had two sizes of scissors, a fat red pincushion that looked like a tomato, an emery bag that looked like a ripe strawberry, and a tape measure that pulled out of a shiny box. When Beezus pushed the button on the box, the tape measure snapped back inside. The box also had needles, pins, and a thimble. Beezus never wore a thimble, but she thought it would be nice to have one in case she ever wanted to use one. "Oh, Aunt Beatrice," she said, "it's the most wonderful sewing box in the whole world. I'll make you two pot holders for Christmas!" Then, as Aunt Beatrice laughed, Beezus clapped her hand over her mouth. The pot holder was supposed to be a surprise.

Ramona had unwrapped a little steam shovel made of red and yellow plastic, which she was now pushing happily around the rug.

Breathlessly Beezus lifted the lid of the second box. "Oh, Aunt Beatrice!" she exclaimed, as she lifted out a dress that was a lovely shade of blue.

"It's just the right shade of blue to match your eyes," explained Aunt Beatrice.

"Is it really?" asked Beezus, delighted that her pretty young aunt liked blue eyes. She was about to tell her about being Sacajawea for the P.T.A. when Father came home from work, and before long dinner was on the table. Mother lit the candles and turned off the dining-room light. How pretty everything looks, thought Beezus. I wish we had candles on the table every night.

After Father had served the chicken and mashed potatoes and peas and Mother had passed the hot rolls, Beezus decided the time had come to tell Aunt Beatrice about being Sacajawea. "Do you know what I did last week?" she began.

"I want some jelly," said Ramona.

"You mean, 'Please pass the jelly,'" corrected Mother, while Beezus waited patiently.

"No, what did you do last week?" asked Aunt Beatrice.

"Well, last week I—" Beezus began again.

"I like purple jelly better than red jelly," said Ramona.

"Ramona, stop interrupting your sister," said Father.

"Well, I *do* like purple jelly better than red jelly," insisted Ramona.

"Never mind," said Mother. "Go on, Beezus."

"Last week—" said Beezus, looking at her aunt, who smiled as if she understood.

"Excuse me, Beezus," Mother cut in. "Ramona, we do not put jelly on our mashed potatoes."

"I like jelly on my mashed potatoes." Ramona stirred potato and jelly around with her fork.

"Ramona, you heard what your mother

said." Father looked stern.

"If I can put butter on my mashed potatoes, why can't I put jelly? I put butter and jelly on toast," said Ramona.

Father couldn't help laughing. "That's a hard question to answer."

"But Mother—" Beezus began.

"I *like* jelly on my mashed potatoes," interrupted Ramona, looking sulky.

"You can't have jelly on your mashed potatoes, because you aren't supposed to," said Beezus crossly, forgetting Sacajawea for the moment.

"That's as good an answer as any," agreed Father. "There are some things we don't do, because we aren't supposed to."

Ramona looked even more sulky.

"Where is my Merry Sunshine?" Mother asked.

Ramona scowled. "I am *too* a Merry Sunshine!" she shouted angrily.

"Ramona," said Mother quietly, "you may go to your room until you can behave yourself."

And serves you right, too, thought Beezus.

"I am *too* a Merry Sunshine," insisted Ramona, but she got down from the table and ran out of the room.

Everyone was silent for a moment. "Beezus, what was it you were trying to tell me?" Aunt Beatrice asked.

And finally Beezus got to tell about leading Lewis and Clark to Oregon, with a doll tied to Mother's breadboard for a papoose, and how her teacher told her what a clever girl she was to think of using a breadboard for a papoose board. Somehow she did not feel the same about telling the story after all Ramona's interruptions. Being Sacajawea for the P.T.A. did not seem very important now. No matter what she did, Ramona always managed to spoil it. Unhappily, Beezus went on eating her chicken and peas. It was another one of those terrible times when she did not love her little sister.

"You mustn't let Ramona get you down," whispered Mother.

Beezus did not answer. What a terrible girl she was not to love her little sister! How shocked and surprised Mother would be if she knew.

"Beezus, you look as if something is bothering you," remarked Aunt Beatrice.

Beezus looked down at her plate. How could she ever tell such an awful thing?

"Why don't you tell us what is wrong?" Aunt Beatrice suggested. "Perhaps we could help."

She sounded so interested and so understanding that Beezus discovered she really wanted to tell what was on her mind. "Sometimes I just don't love Ramona!" she blurted out, to get it over with. There! She had said it right out loud. And on her birthday, too. Now everyone would know what a terrible girl she was.

"My goodness, is that all that bothers you?" Mother sounded surprised.

Beezus nodded miserably.

"Why, there's no reason why you *should* love Ramona all the time," Mother went on. "After all, there are probably lots of times when she doesn't love you."

Now it was Beezus's turn to be surprised—surprised and relieved at the same time. She wondered why she hadn't thought of it that way before.

Aunt Beatrice smiled. "Dorothy," she said to Mother, "do you remember the time I—" She began to laugh so hard she couldn't finish the sentence.

"You took my doll with the beautiful yellow curls and dyed her hair with black shoe dye," finished Mother, and the two grown-up sisters went into gales of laughter. "I didn't love you a bit that time," admitted Mother. "I was mad at you for days."

"And you were always so bossy, because you were older," said Aunt Beatrice. "I'm sure I didn't love you at all when you were supposed to take me to school and made me walk about six feet behind you, because you didn't want people to know you had to look after me."

"Mother!" exclaimed Beezus in shocked delight.

"Did I do that?" laughed Mother. "I had forgotten all about it."

"What else did Mother do?" Beezus asked eagerly.

"She was terribly fussy," said Aunt Beatrice. "We had to share a room and she used to get mad because I was untidy. Once she threw all my paper dolls into the wastebasket, because I had left them on her side of the dresser. That was another time we didn't love each other."

Fascinated, Beezus hoped this interesting conversation would continue. Imagine Mother and Aunt Beatrice quarreling!

"Oh, but the worst thing of all!" said Mother. "Remember—"

"I'll never forget!" exclaimed Aunt Beatrice, as if she knew what Mother was talking about. "Wasn't I awful?"

"Perfectly terrible," agreed Mother, wiping her eyes because she was laughing so hard.

"What happened?" begged Beezus, who could not wait to find out what dreadful thing Aunt Beatrice had done when she was a girl. "Mother, tell what happened."

"It all began when the girls began to take autograph albums to school," began Mother and then went off into another fit of laughter. "Oh, Beatrice, you tell it."

"Of course I wanted an autograph album

too," continued Aunt Beatrice. Beezus nodded, because she, too, had an autograph album. "Well, your mother, who was always very sensible, saved her allowance and bought a beautiful album with a red cover stamped in gold. How I envied her!"

"As soon as your Aunt Beatrice got her allowance she always ran right over to the school store and spent it," added Mother.

"Yes, and on the most awful junk," agreed Aunt Beatrice. "Licorice whips, and pencils that were square instead of round, and I don't know what all."

"Yes, but what about the autograph album?" Beezus asked.

"Well, when I—oh, I'm almost ashamed to tell it," said Aunt Beatrice.

"Oh, go on," urged Mother. "It's priceless."

"Well, when I saw your mother with that brand-new autograph album that she bought, because she was so sensible, I was annoyed, because I wanted one too and I hadn't saved my allowance. And then she asked me if I'd like to sign my name in it."

"It was my night to set the table," added Mother. "I never should have left her alone with it."

"But what happened?" Beezus could hardly wait to find out.

"I sat down at the desk and picked up a pen, planning to write on the last page, 'By hook or by crook I'll be the last in your book,'" said Aunt Beatrice.

"Oh, did people write that in those days, too?" Beezus was surprised, because she had thought this was something very new to write in an autograph album.

"But I didn't write it," continued Aunt Beatrice. "I just sat there wishing I had an autograph album, and then I took the pen and wrote my name on every single page in the book!"

"Aunt Beatrice! You didn't! Not in Mother's brand-new autograph album!" Beezus was horrified and delighted at the same time. What a terrible thing to do!

"She certainly did," said Mother, "and not just plain Beatrice Haswell, either. She wrote Beatrice Ann Haswell, Miss Bea Haswell, B. A. Haswell, Esquire, and everything she could think of. When she couldn't think of any more ways to write her name she started all over again."

"Oh, Aunt Beatrice, how perfectly awful," exclaimed Beezus, with a touch of admiration in her voice.

"Yes, wasn't it?" agreed Aunt Beatrice. "I don't know what got into me."

"And what did Mother do?" inquired Beezus, eager for the whole story.

"We had a dreadful quarrel and I got spanked," said Aunt Beatrice. "Your mother didn't love me one little bit for a long, long time. And I wouldn't admit it, but I felt terrible because I had spoiled her autograph album. Fortunately Christmas came along about that time and we were both given albums and that put an end to the whole thing."

Why, thought Beezus, Aunt Beatrice used to be every bit as awful as Ramona. And yet look how nice she is now. Beezus could scarcely believe it. And now Mother and Aunt Beatrice, who had quarreled when they were girls, loved each other and thought the things they had done were funny! They actually laughed about it. Well, maybe when she was grown up she would think it was funny that Ramona had put eggshells in one birthday cake and baked her rubber doll with another. Maybe she wouldn't think Ramona was so exasperating, after all. Maybe that was just the way things were with sisters. A lovely feeling of relief came over Beezus. What if she *didn't* love Ramona all the time? It didn't matter at all. She was just like any other sister.

"Mother," whispered Beezus, happier than she had felt in a long time, "I hope Ramona comes back before we have my birthday cake."

"Don't worry," Mother said, smiling. "I'm sure she wouldn't miss it for anything."

And sure enough, in a few minutes Ramona appeared from the bedroom and took her place at the table. "I can behave myself," she said.

"It's about time," observed Father.

Beezus watched Ramona eating her cold mashed potatoes and jelly and thought how much easier things would be now that she could look at her sister when she was exasperating and think, Ha-ha, Ramona, this is one of those times when I don't have to love you.

"Girls with birthdays don't have to help clear the table," said Mother, beginning to carry out the dishes.

Beezus waited expectantly for the most important moment of the day. She heard her mother take the cake out of its box and strike a match to light the candles. "Oh," she breathed happily, when Mother appeared in the doorway with the cake in her hands. It

was the most beautiful cake she had ever seen—pink with a wreath of white roses made of icing, and ten pink candles that threw a soft glowing light on Mother's face.

"'Happy birthday to you,'" sang Mother and Father and Aunt Beatrice and Ramona. "'Happy birthday, dear Beezus, happy birthday to you.'"

"Make a wish," said Father.

Beezus paused a minute. Then she closed her eyes and thought, I wish all my birthdays would turn out to be as wonderful as this one finally did. She opened her eyes and blew as hard as she could.

"Your wish is granted!" cried Aunt Beatrice, smiling across the ten smoking candles.

"'Happy birthday, dear Beezus, happy birthday to you!'" sang Ramona at the top of her voice.

"All right, Ramona," said Mother with a

touch of exasperation in her voice. "Once is enough."

But at that moment Beezus did not think her little sister was exasperating at all.

BEVERLY CLEARY is one of America's most popular authors. Born in McMinnville, Oregon, she lived on a farm in Yamhill until she was six and then moved to Portland. After college, as the children's librarian in Yakima, Washington, she was challenged to find stories for non-readers. She wrote her first book, HENRY HUGGINS, in response to a boy's question, "Where are the books about kids like us?"

Mrs. Cleary's books have earned her many prestigious awards, including the American Library Association's Laura Ingalls Wilder Award, presented in recognition of her lasting contribution to children's literature. Her DEAR MR. HENSHAW was awarded the 1984 John Newbery Medal, and both RAMONA QUIMBY, AGE 8 and RAMONA AND HER FATHER have been named Newbery Honor Books. In addition, her books have won more than thirty-five statewide awards based on the votes of her young readers. Her characters, including Henry Huggins, Ellen Tebbits, Otis Spofford, and Beezus and Ramona Quimby, as well as Ribsy, Socks, and Ralph S. Mouse, have delighted children for generations. Mrs. Cleary lives in coastal California.

Visit Beverly Cleary on the World Wide Web at
www.beverlycleary.com.

1

Ramona's Great Day

"I am *not* a pest," Ramona Quimby told her big sister Beezus.

"Then stop acting like a pest," said Beezus, whose real name was Beatrice. She was standing by the front window waiting for her friend Mary Jane to walk to school with her.

"I'm not acting like a pest. I'm singing and skipping," said Ramona, who had only recently learned to skip with both feet. Ramona did not think she was a pest. No matter what others said, she never thought she was a pest. The people who called her a pest were always bigger and so they could be unfair.

Ramona went on with her singing and skipping. "This is a great day, a great day, a great day!" she sang, and to Ramona, who was feeling grown up in a dress instead of play clothes, this was a great day, the greatest day of her whole life. No longer would she have to sit on her tricycle watching Beezus and Henry Huggins and the rest of the boys and girls in the neighborhood go off to school. Today she was going to school, too. Today she was going to learn to read and write and do all the things that would help her catch up with Beezus.

"Come *on*, Mama!" urged Ramona, pausing in her singing and skipping. "We don't

want to be late for school."

"Don't pester, Ramona," said Mrs.
Quimby. "I'll get you there in plenty of time."

"I'm *not* pestering," protested Ramona,
who never meant to pester. She was not a
slowpoke grown-up. She was a girl who

could not wait. Life was so interesting she had to find out what happened next.

Then Mary Jane arrived. "Mrs. Quimby, would it be all right if Beezus and I take Ramona to kindergarten?" she asked.

"No!" said Ramona instantly. Mary Jane was one of those girls who always wanted to pretend she was a mother and who always wanted Ramona to be the baby. Nobody was going to catch Ramona being a baby on her first day of school.

"Why not?" Mrs. Quimby asked Ramona. "You could walk to school with Beezus and Mary Jane just like a big girl."

"No, I couldn't." Ramona was not fooled for an instant. Mary Jane would talk in that silly voice she used when she was being a mother and take her by the hand and help her across the street, and everyone would think she really was a baby.

"Please, Ramona," coaxed Beezus. "It

4

would be lots of fun to take you in and introduce you to the kindergarten teacher."

"No!" said Ramona, and stamped her foot. Beczus and Mary Jane might have fun, but she wouldn't. Nobody but a genuine grown-up was going to take her to school. If she had to, she would make a great big noisy fuss, and when Ramona made a great big noisy fuss, she usually got her own way. Great big noisy fusses were often necessary when a girl was the youngest member of the family and the youngest person on her block.

"All right, Ramona," said Mrs. Quimby. "Don't make a great big noisy fuss. If that's the way you feel about it, you don't have to walk with the girls. I'll take you."

"Hurry, Mama," said Ramona happily, as she watched Beezus and Mary Jane go out the door. But when Ramona finally got her mother out of the house, she was disappointed to see one of her mother's friends,

Mrs. Kemp, approaching with her son Howie and his little sister Willa Jean, who was riding in a stroller. "Hurry, Mama," urged Ramona, not wanting to wait for the Kemps. Because their mothers were friends, she and Howie were expected to get along with one another.

"Hi, there!" Mrs. Kemp called out, so of course Ramona's mother had to wait.

Howie stared at Ramona. He did not like having to get along with her any more than she liked having to get along with him.

Ramona stared back. Howie was a solid-looking boy with curly blond hair. ("Such a waste on a boy," his mother often remarked.) The legs of his new jeans were turned up, and he was wearing a new shirt with long sleeves. He did not look the least bit excited about starting kindergarten. That was the trouble with Howie, Ramona felt. He never got excited. Straight-haired Willa Jean, who was interesting to Ramona because she was so sloppy, blew out a mouthful of wet zwieback crumbs and laughed at her cleverness.

"Today my baby leaves me," remarked Mrs. Quimby with a smile, as the little group proceeded down Klickitat Street toward Glenwood School.

Ramona, who enjoyed being her mother's baby, did not enjoy being called her mother's baby, especially in front of Howie.

"They grow up quickly," observed Mrs. Kemp.

Ramona could not understand why grown-ups always talked about how quickly children grew up. Ramona thought growing up was the slowest thing there was, slower even than waiting for Christmas to come. She had been waiting years just to get to kindergarten, and the last half hour was the slowest part of all.

When the group reached the intersection

nearest Glenwood School, Ramona was pleased to see that Beezus's friend Henry Huggins was the traffic boy in charge of that particular corner. After Henry had led them across the street, Ramona ran off toward the kindergarten, which was a temporary wooden building with its own playground. Mothers and children were already entering the open door. Some of the children looked frightened, and one girl was crying.

"We're late!" cried Ramona. "Hurry!"

Howie was not a boy to be hurried. "I don't see any tricycles," he said critically. "I don't see any dirt to dig in."

Ramona was scornful. "This isn't nursery school. Tricycles and dirt are for nursery school." Her own tricycle was hidden in the garage, because it was too babyish for her now that she was going to school.

Some big first-grade boys ran past yelling, "Kindergarten babies! Kindergarten babies!"

"We are *not* babies!" Ramona yelled back, as she led her mother into the kindergarten. Once inside she stayed close to her. Everything was so strange, and there was so much to see: the little tables and chairs; the row of cupboards, each with a different picture on the door; the play stove; and the wooden blocks big enough to stand on.

The teacher, who was new to Glenwood School, turned out to be so young and pretty she could not have been a grown-up very long. It was rumored she had never taught school before. "Hello, Ramona. My name is Miss Binney," she said, speaking each syllable distinctly as she pinned Ramona's name to her dress. "I am so glad you have come to kindergarten." Then she took Ramona by the hand and led her to one of the little tables and chairs. "Sit here for the present," she said with a smile.

A present! thought Ramona, and knew at

once she was going to like Miss Binney.

"Good-by, Ramona," said Mrs. Quimby. "Be a good girl."

As she watched her mother walk out the door, Ramona decided school was going to be even better than she had hoped. Nobody had told her she was going to get a present the very first day. What kind of present could it be, she wondered, trying to remember if Beezus had ever been given a present by her teacher.

Ramona listened carefully while Miss Binney showed Howie to a table, but all her teacher said was, "Howie, I would like you to sit here." Well! thought Ramona. Not everyone is going to get a present so Miss Binney must like me best. Ramona watched and listened as the other boys and girls arrived, but Miss Binney did not tell anyone else he was going to get a present if he sat in a certain chair. Ramona wondered if her present would be wrapped in fancy paper and tied with a ribbon like a birthday present. She hoped so.

As Ramona sat waiting for her present she watched the other children being introduced to Miss Binney by their mothers. She found two members of the morning kindergarten especially interesting. One was a boy named Davy, who was small, thin, and eager. He was the only boy in the class in short pants, and Ramona liked him at once. She liked him so much she decided she would like to kiss him.

The other interesting person was a big girl named Susan. Susan's hair looked like the hair on the girls in the pictures of the old-fashioned stories Beezus liked to read. It was reddish-brown and hung in curls like springs that touched her shoulders and bounced as she walked. Ramona had never seen such curls before. All the curly-haired girls she knew wore their hair short. Ramona put her hand to her own short straight hair, which was an ordinary brown, and longed to touch that bright springy hair. She longed to stretch one of those curls and watch it spring back. *Boing!* thought Ramona, making a mental noise like a spring on a television cartoon and wishing for thick, springy *boing-boing* hair like Susan's.